THE INSTITUTE FOR TAXI POETRY

Joti, 18.04.2012

NcR.

The Institute for Taxi Poetry

IMRAAN COOVADIA

UMUZI

Published in 2012 by Umuzi
an imprint of Random House Struik (Pty) Ltd
Company Reg No 1966/003153/07
First Floor, Wembley Square, Solan Road,
Cape Town, 8001, South Africa
PO Box 1144, Cape Town, 8000, South Africa
umuzi@randomstruik.co.za
www.randomstruik.co.za

First edition, first printing 2012
1 3 5 7 9 8 6 4 2

ISBN 978-1-4152-0165-7 (Print)
ISBN 978-1-4152-0458-0 (ePub)
ISBN 978-1-4152-0459-7 (PDF)

Cover design by Joey Hi-Fi
Text design by 128Design
Author photograph by Gerhard Müller
Set in Sabon 11 on 15 pt

Printed and bound in South Africa by Paarlmedia,
Jan van Riebeeck Avenue, Paarl

I travel on your black and white and roboted roads
Through your thick iron breath.

— MONGANE WALLY SEROTE,
"The City Johannesburg"

MONDAY

~

PROBLEM #1: There was a cat, Marmalade, who was out of his mind. Plus, Solly Greenfields, the only friend I could bear, had been shot dead in his railway cottage near Woodstock Main Road. If you told me I was in for the most complicated week of my life, then I couldn't contradict you on that. But I might try.

When I went to Solly's funeral Monday, I thought nobody had a solid reason to do him in. He was an old man, which meant his adversaries were also getting on. The taxi companies had never forgiven him for starting the Road Safety Council. Yet that was years ago. I hadn't heard about any new enemies. Solly would have been proud to mention them. He had been quiet recently, content with the trouble he earned over a lifetime as a great taxi poet. I was among the first of Solly's interns, by the way, and maybe not the one who displeased him the most, and maybe that was the closest either of us came to a proper relationship.

Who would kill Solly? There were no obvious suspects. Two bullets had been found in the wall in the corridor of the house. They had to be dug out of the old plaster. The other bullets were in the victim, who was discovered in his dressing gown, lying on the couch with the scuffed purple buttons, which stood in the corner of the lounge. The bathtub was slopping full of cold water, and the needle of the record player was caught on a Dollar Brand album.

The tub would be full. It was the temple of Solly's domestic existence, surrounded by the red and green hotel soaps left over from a rare period of formal employment. He got into the bath when visitors were around, especially his interns. He was so heavy that you expected the porcelain tub to rock back and forth on its iron feet. But that didn't prevent him from removing his clothes at the drop of a hat. For a fat old man, he wasn't ashamed to be naked and, in fact, he was finicky about the condition of his skin, from his freckled neck to his feet.

Solly's neck got thinner and stronger and redder as he got older until it was the most vigorous thing about him. The crime rate meant you had to be tough to live in that area—Woodstock, Salt River, Observatory, and the warehouses interspersed with concrete blocks of flats between the railway line and the harbour. There was no waiting for the car from the security company to arrive. You had to be prepared for self-defence. When somebody crossed onto Solly's property in the Woodstock way, on the way to somewhere else or just to check if there was anything on the premises worth taking, Solly pushed the offender out of the gate, flexing his neck like a dilapidated bull. He didn't fear to get knifed. Right to the end there was this fearless quality which crackled out of him, like electricity, and which he provoked in his interns in the field of taxi poetry.

In his seventies, Solly was crammed with projects, and thoughts, and burning pleasures, and hatreds which burned just as high, right to the top of his brown old head. He planned to expand the Road Safety Council, which had become little more than Solly himself, some students and the pamphlets they printed on their famous silk-screen machine borrowed from a government school during a teachers' strike never to be returned. He also wanted to set out his objections to the whole existence of the Perreira Institute and its claim to produce taxi poets as if they were sausages. He had discussed a potential memoir on the inception of taxi poetry, judging his own contribution, Geromian's, and the good old cause of the revolution which had never begun and would never therefore be concluded. He even said something about falling in love, but I wasn't even sure there was someone.

For Solly, taxi poetry was a way of life. There was a code which he subscribed to. It was the only type of honour which made sense to me. I couldn't imagine who would put three, or five, bullets into such an honourable man.

It was a point of honour for me, on Solly's behalf, to take Marmalade, who had been discovered on the top shelf in the ironing cupboard after the body had been removed from the house. He had one scrappy orange ear, and an untorn white one which he sheared away from presenting to you.

Solly never composed a taxi poem without one or both of his hands on Marmalade and the bad ear which he reluctantly allowed you to touch. The cat wasn't in good shape. His belly dragged on the carpet as he moved suspiciously around my flat. He shed his orange hair in vast quantities and hunted invisible insects. This Marmalade was out of his mind but I had a good understanding of how he saw things.

I happen to be a taxi poet—a former taxi poet according to some—in a city run by Croatian disco men from Zagreb and Malay gangsters from Pinelands, by publicity girls wearing long earrings, by dollar millionaires with business connections to the ruling Congress Party, by old Trotskyites and Bukharinites, and by cabinet ministers and dictators from elsewhere who reside along the Atlantic seaboard or on the wine estates inland.

Solly Greenfields—who had once been a taxi poet, and then a Buddhist, once a Muslim, once a Jew, once a lowly cook in a grease-sprayed apron in the room-service kitchen of the Mount Nelson, on other occasions a guest in the very same hotel—wasn't the first to go. If he happened to be the last then it was only because the world was about to end.

Was there a pattern? I wasn't sure. There wasn't necessarily a plan to bump off taxi poets. In Cape Town nobody had a plan. We made arrangements one day at a time because the day after tomorrow was impossible to predict. It wasn't certain there would be such a day.

So what can I tell you? So there happened to be a lot of lead flying around. So there happened to be a lot of taxi poets in the way.

Given his more private life in recent years, there were more people at the funeral than I anticipated. This included Parker, of course, the taxi boss for whom I once worked, in a different life, but many others as well.

Many people regarded Solly as a dear friend. In his way, he reciprocated. Yet he didn't talk so much about absent friends. He didn't live in his memories, didn't expend his energy wishing for what could have been and what would come to be regardless. You wouldn't describe him as sentimental. Neither was he cold, in person.

You could see from the ceremony. Gathered here in Parow was such a mixture of types whose hearts Solly touched—sliding-door men, members of the garment union who fought hand in hand with

Solly against Chinese imports, others from fishing villages on the West Coast who had graph-paper faces, as well as the technikon philosophers, and math teachers, and a township beauty queen, one of those who stepped out of a tin shack in a satin ballroom dress, who had recited a taxi poem by Solly on the occasion of her matric dance.

There were the usual personages from Congress and the municipality. The taxi companies, despite their dislike for rules and regulations, were close to the ruling party. They had a common interest in the public tenders which ran into the billions.

It was even said that the government was a giant taxi company. Whereas I thought, that was making a simple thing out of a complicated one. God gave us brains because he didn't care to make the world straightforward.

The burial was soon underway. A man in an untucked blue shirt read out some verses from a cloth-covered book. He wore high-heeled shoes underneath his loose white trousers. Although he was quite young, he sported a fierce black beard. I could tell that he knew what he was proclaiming by heart, and was only presenting the book for show.

The men from the Greenfields family passed the spades from one to the other so each man had the chance to shovel soil onto the body. They worked without talking. None of them, to look at their faces, reminded me of the deceased man. Solly's vegetable features, his cucumbery nose and hothouse brow were his own.

I thought it was unjust that the Greenfields clan had such a prominent role in the proceedings. I didn't trust them. They ran a chain of discount clothing shops. As cousins, or uncles, or nephews, or even as brothers, they never had much to do with Solly, the living, breathing, coughing, and spitting human being, the man who rode in Bedford trucks before there were Toyotas.

I wasn't sure what the grudge was between Solly and his relations, what facts lay between them, and why they rarely, if ever, invited him into their houses. But there was something. I hadn't once seen them turn up at his hedge. They never recited a line of his taxi poetry, or conversed with a single one of his interns and discovered how their family connection, Solly, showed us the gates to the universe.

The feeling was mutual, as most feelings are. The Greenfields family had been irrelevant to Solly's existence. He had followed his independent principles, and his instincts. They took him far away from his point of origin. Now he was dead, of course, the relatives were the ones holding all the spades.

Behind them, on the building lot opposite the cemetery, a truck was offloading gravel. It hissed as it fell. It mounted into a cone while the driver shouted from the high window of his cab. I could hear the gravel. I couldn't hear the driver. He was shouting although across the road I couldn't catch his voice, only observe the angry and determined workings of his mouth. From it came a wind which couldn't be heard.

The diggers finished their work before Parker noticed me. He wasn't pleased to see me, nor do I think he was displeased. Once many people thought we were close, almost like father and son, although the closeness between us had subsequently vanished.

I couldn't place my finger on when the change took place. The fault lay on my side. I had these rough edges, and sharp elbows, which I couldn't always control. They were often grating on somebody, or, unbeknownst to me, pressing hard into somebody's side. It wasn't a tragedy. Solly said you must accept that the current united you with some people while dividing you from others, just as a boat was carried along and passed different points along the bank.

I was prepared to be ignored by Parker, but after ten minutes he came towards me. His guards, the new ones who didn't know anything about the development of the transport industry, followed behind him. I didn't recognise them. They were new but they weren't an improvement on before, a rule which, in my opinion, summed up the length of recorded history.

Parker himself was fatter than I remembered, perhaps the result of the progress of the diabetes. His mole, the one on the side of his face, was enormous and at its centre stood a buggish black hair. He moved slowly. He wore a long grey linen jacket, a style I had not seen on him before. It did something, but not very much, to conceal the larger size of his trunk, as if a magician had attempted to make Parker disappear and had been stopped in the middle of the trick. There was no spell to make the distance between us disappear.

"How are you, my old friend Adam Ravens? It's years since I saw you last. You were the thinnest employee I ever had, a bean stalk. You've put on some weight."

"Parker, I take it as a compliment," I said. "Sometimes I even miss my former life in your taxis. By the way, this isn't the first time we see each other. I greeted you last year, just for one second, at the celebration of the Congress Party's centenary. Solly insisted I accompany him. He still had friends in the Party from the old days."

"Well, I am sorry we meet again under these circumstances. Solly should have been celebrating his century rather than the Congress Party which has done so little for us. Tell me, how is Zebulon? I haven't seen him since he was this high."

"He's good, despite being at the age when communication is impossible. He doesn't want to talk and can't see the point of listening. You remember that, as a child, he would wheeze because of asthma, and keep us up throughout the night. Now he's already taller than me, by half a foot almost. He can smoke cloves because his breathing is now perfect. And, you know, Zeb suddenly has a life of his own, his own friends and worries. He wants to be a sliding-door man and drop out of the university."

Parker opened his linen jacket to reveal the pink lining and two buttons sewn onto the pocket. Inside it he was bigger, and more broken down, than I'd previously judged.

"You send him to me, Adam. I have an interest in the young people of today. I am still attached to his father. I won't lie. I can't forget that you had the honesty to tell me things to my face when nobody else would have dared. You weren't definitively correct, but it showed your honesty, similar to Solly's. And this is something I remember. When they told me you were on the staff of this new Institute I immediately wrote a cheque. And otherwise what do you have to say?"

"I can't complain." I thought about it. Under the circumstances, it seemed like the wrong thing to say. "At least I am not bad in my own life. The business with Solly hit me hard. For me, without him, this place cannot claim to have a moral centre."

"No, for me also. Don't forget that we grew up almost on the same street. The Greenfields were a legendary family in Woodstock, as you know. Although Solly's father was only a boilermaker, later to be an official fitter and turner, he was also a reader, and a thinking person, and a leader in the community. His door was always open to us. Then Solly and I were in the same class at commercial school, even if I wasn't in the same league as a scholar. We bought White Rabbits together from the Chinese shop there. Many years ago, when Solly told me to put you in as a sliding-door man, I did not hesitate. But I am preaching to the converted. Something you don't know, probably, is that Solly composed a verse when I got married for the first time. The second and the third time he refused."

"I didn't know that."

"It's a true fact. He said marriages may not be unique but his verses had to be. So, in a way, he had something to teach me too. Still and all, the relationship went in both directions. I supplied his family with petrol on the cheap, when it became scarce. I did a lot for the Greenfields, whether or not they choose to acknowledge it. I don't know how many of the people here can claim to know Solly equally well. Apart from his brothers, who are putting in an appearance today, there is nobody who enjoyed such a relationship with Solly Greenfields as you and I did."

There was nobody here who understood the phenomenon of Solly Greenfields, not even Parker, chairman of the Taxi Owners Association. Once upon a time I rode around in a 2.2 litre Toyota Hi-Ace, the model with the reinforced side step, which belonged to Parker. On Solly's recommendation I had the task of recording the sayings and doings of the employees, from the drivers to the sliding-door men to the mechanics who worked for his taxi company.

Despite the socialist tendency of the government, transportation was mostly in the private sector. There was big money involved. Taxi companies operated the minibuses which carried most commuters in and out of town. Their workhorse was the Hi-Ace, big enough to seat twelve passengers in safety, up to twenty-six not so very safely, and up to forty if it was being used for a wedding or to bus voters to the polls on Election Day.

The Taxi Owners Association united the various companies under one heading. It did everything necessary to keep people moving, assigning routes to each company, collecting rates, providing security, negotiating with the relevant Congress Party structures, and renting space for taxi ranks in town. It also paid gunmen to run off any unlicensed operators. The owners of the taxi companies hired and fired their drivers and sliding-door men, and complained about their labour force just like any old capitalist. All of this taken together meant that regional transportation, and therefore our travelling form of life, was different from anywhere else on the great globe.

Then there were the taxi poets and our contribution. I never took the responsibility of being one lightly. No taxi poet worthy of the name would. For there was nobody to predict the future of a taxi poem. It might be as transitory as the career of a summer's fly, or it might remain in circulation for a season, a decade, or a day of Brahma, far longer than the Hi-Ace on which a taxi poem was stencilled.

In my day, half of Parker's taxis were in the most severe state of disrepair. Whoever drove them knew how to handle a steering column stripped down to the skeletal arm of the coupling. But they kept running. Toyota designed the Hi-Ace for the condition of our roads, to endure despite how the drivers used them twenty hours of the day, and how the owners used the drivers. Nonetheless, in my view, we taxi poets built our products better than the Toyota Motor Corporation.

In 1995 or thereabouts, a taxi poet was somebody to be reckoned with. It was some consolation to the Hi-Ace driver to relate his name and circumstances to me. He had the hope that his story would be painted on the side of his same minibus, and perhaps chalked between the posters for music shows and cellphone plans on one of the buildings on Grand Parade, by the main taxi rank, and in this way continue to circulate through the community. The same driver or sliding-door man, who cared in no apparent way for his family or neighbourhood or religion, cared that they should remember his name in the event of his premature death, which, in 1995, came as often as not.

There were fortunes to be made and to be lost and to be taken away in this youngest great industry in the youngest corner of the world. Someone who borrowed from Standard Bank for one minibus rose in a few years to fabulous riches, and the ownership of a dozen taxis. You created your own opportunities, sometimes by disposing of the person next in line. Parker knew how it worked because it was the story of his own career.

He was standing now talking to me but looking across to the other side of the grave, where they had cemented broken bottles on the top of the brick wall to prevent access from the adjacent block of flats.

"Loyalty is for life. I never criticised your keeping-it-cool attitude. You wanted to leave the company? That is your affair. In the world today, people come and go. What I don't accept is that you leave my friendship behind."

"I wouldn't dream of it."

"There's a meeting Wednesday. Come to that. You can meet the other members of the Taxi Owners Association. There is every reason for somebody in your position, at this Institute of yours, to have friends in the right places." Parker searched inside his jacket for his cellphone, which was ringing. He got it out, studied the radiant blue screen like a scholar, then didn't open it. "We can pick up where we left off on Wednesday. You are so used to causing trouble that you forget your real value."

"How's that?"

"Ah, you know just as well as I do. As a taxi poet, like Solly, you have a different view on the world. I mean, even if it's just the simplest of things. You can see things from one angle, and then from a different angle." Parker touched the brown-suede mole on the side of his face. I envied his freedom. He seemed to want to continue talking, as if there was something that needed to be worked out inside himself. "With Solly, I could discuss all the topics under the sun, whether it was Cleopatra or Prince Valiant comics or Trotsky's Mexico years or the new style in Lucky Packets or the poetry of Khalil Gibran, which he could never tolerate despite my arguments. I believe there was nowhere Solly's mind couldn't reach, from the lowest to the highest. Now he has been snuffed out."

"Funny how that keeps happening."

I could have angered my former boss. I was patiently digging my own grave. Indeed, when I started as a driver in a Parker's taxi, my employer reminded me of a spade with a long handle. Ten years had passed since I even worked for the company. But I knew the score and not one note in it had changed.

Taxi companies looked simple, operating clapped-out Hi-Aces and employing, as they did, little more than children from the informal settlements as drivers and general dogs' bodies, making small money carrying nurses and shop assistants and building-site foremen to and from town. Contrary to appearances, the companies took a sophisticated view of their economic interests. As private entities, they expressed a sceptical view of parastatals, like Transnet, which managed the trains and port facilities, and the Golden Arrow Bus Service, which itself was owned by the investment arm of the giant trade union.

It was only when the public companies poached too many passengers that radical action was forced on the Taxi Owners Association. Late some evening, the train yards and bus stations got served with round after round of Molotov cocktails, flaming rags stuck in their bottled mouths. They were the same revolution-ary cocktails which had been served to the old government but with a different message on their burning tongues.

The fires burned for a week. Someone poured sugar into the diesel caps of the Golden Arrow buses. Shots flew at the main railway link opposite Game Discount World. The economy stopped turning over, from the canning plants in Salt River to the wholesale wine shops and tile warehouses on Paarden Eiland. Trainloads of coal, bound for the power station in Athlone, built up in the Wellington and Simon's Town depots. The lights began to go out.

Eventually some element in Congress brokered a truce between the antagonists. The price of a third-class ticket increased to cover the wrecked buses and locomotives. Transnet shelved its expansion plans. The Golden Arrow Bus Service laid off a dozen drivers and cancelled its routes through the politically sensitive regions of the Cape Flats.

Everybody who amounted to somebody in the scheme of things came out golden. Everybody, who was nobody whose opinion mattered, paid extra and walked five hundred yards out of his way to the nearest taxi rank instead of to the bus stop on the corner. Dockets were issued for the sake of formality, but nobody ever showed up in court on arson charges.

That's how big business operated at the Cape. The taxi companies were big business and made big profits, whether we considered their revenue books, or checked in the glove compartment of one of their Hi-Aces. Ninety percent of the local drug traffic—tik and those long pink-and-white Mandrax capsules which separate a man and his wits for a weekend—circulated on the minibuses. Needless to say, the taxi companies were the most substantial patrons of transport poetry in the region.

Do I have a point? To reach the top of the transport sector, in the turbulent universe of the taxi industry, was a Darwinian effort. One in a thousand survived. Only cunning and tough-minded types ran a proper company, keeping the drivers from wrecking the vehicles, restraining the sliding-door men from pocketing the cash, and sustaining the depredations of the Congress Party plus municipal policemen in search of cold-drink money in the morning and lunch money thereafter.

If you were a taxi boss, like Parker, you were nobody's fool, not even your own, which was my favourite kind. For instance, as the administrator of a taxi association, you knew that virtues and vices differed in magnitude and direction from one individual to the next. You understood that finding out someone's vices was like obtaining the pin number for his soul.

My vice—my secret pin which I should never reveal and never

write down on a piece of paper like this—was getting in the last word. I didn't intend to trouble other people, only to enlighten them. On the majority of Mondays and Sundays and Thursdays and Wednesdays, and some other days of the week, I felt closer to the truth than most other people, and closer, in fact, than anyone but Solly Greenfields.

Granted: this conviction of mine had the potential to create bitterness. But silence, and compliance, any form or type of submission, were antithetical to the mission of a taxi poet. I preferred that others submit, instead, to the crackle of whatever truth flowed through me like the sparks at Parker's house in Belthorn Estate where they electrocuted many a sliding-door man who had slid away from financial morality. It was even possible that torturers, and truth seekers, and transport poets were united in pursuit of this strange crackle.

On this one occasion, at Solly's funeral, Parker indulged me in my vice. He didn't come back at me. It made me suspicious. My presence wasn't so sweet for Parker, considering our history. He wanted something more.

There was nothing I had to give except my silver tongue, which wasn't so silver. I had Marmalade, and some of Solly's records I had borrowed, Dollar Brand and Miriam Makeba. Then there was Zebulon, my son, who hadn't spoken to me in five days and seven hours, and my position at the Jose da Silva Perreira Institute for Taxi Poetry, which I could lose on any day. Nobody even wanted my secrets. I wasn't sure I had a true friend in the world now that Solly was gone. As for self-pity, which I had enough to lend, every person has his own portion and doesn't need to borrow.

I won't say Parker was pleased by our encounter at Solly's funeral. He pursed his mouth, which was as black as liquorice, and trembled for a minute. He wanted to speak his mind, tell me where to get off, or maybe his sugar was low. For a minute I thought he was going to slap me right there and then. I didn't see what I had done to make him so angry. His temper must have worsened.

For some reason I wanted to touch the brown-suede mole on the side of Parker's face and feel its chicken-foot texture on the palm of my hand. I would have registered that its surface was as hot as a blood vessel and that it rose and fell, rose, and fell, with his pulse. I would have been the first man to touch him on the face in fifty years. If being a taxi poet meant one thing, it meant doing things without exact reasons, and even being prepared to die, if necessary, to bring a new sensation into existence.

If he had been there, Solly Greenfields would have done it himself. He was the one person who could joust with Parker on equal terms, and he would never back down. I couldn't afford to be as fearless as Solly and maybe, in the end, I had no right to count myself a member of the same profession. Solly was a martyr to the cause of taxi poetry, and I had the impulse to prod Parker and hound him until he told me whatever he happened to know about the case. There wasn't much that escaped the attention of a taxi boss, especially if a friend was involved.

However, Parker turned back to his cellphone. I was dismissed, having received an invitation for Wednesday it would be ticklish to refuse. I would have to go to Belthorn Estate even though, as a member of staff at the university and as someone engaged in training new things, I wanted nothing more than to stay clear of Parker's company, and, in general, the taxi world.

So ten years ago I worked for Parker and did the rounds in his minibuses. So we used to be close. As usual, nobody could say where the years had all flown. Maybe the same place the old moon went.

When the grave had been filled I went and stood there at the side. Someone was combing the soil with a rake, making it level. There were small white pebbles in the ground.

The mourners were dispersing as I waited. Parker and Montalban, all Solly's brothers and uncles and nephews, vanished to their transportation. Many of them would walk to the pick-up on Voortrekker Road where there was a betting parlour for the horses with bulletproof glass above the counter. From there the funeralgoers would return to Woodstock and the family house, decorated with black crepe over the interior doors, where Solly never went out of free will.

It was good to have my friend to myself. I knelt down and put my hands on top of the plot. The ground was cold, loamy, not quite hard. It was full of worms, mining their inch-long claims. I imagined them nosing at his strong old red neck and his chest and legs, which were covered with crops of white hair.

Solly had wanted very much to be buried here—I mean, if he had to be buried at all, and if not on the dingy margin of Parow, then in the general area, somewhere between the Hottentots-Holland mountains and the Sea Point Pick n Pay, the most hospitable place for the species, he believed, and, not coincidentally, the best place to be a transport poet who expressed the travelling character of humanity.

In his own words:

I did wish for some boots, strong like Dunlop rubber,
To walk the road back north, to where there is a parking lot
Beside my heart which I buried there,
To where there is an empty spot, Audi-shaped.

If Solly, nudged by the worms, had risen out of his sheet he would have marvelled at his good fortune. The same clichés everyone repeated found a place in his heart also. You would have thought, as a taxi poet, he could create his own.

But Solly, who wouldn't tolerate a cliché on the side of a taxi, adored the clichés of daily life, from the cheap snoek, wrapped in newspaper like an engine part, to the Cape Town mebos, dried and sugared fruit available from the corner cafés in Rylands, as well as the no-name-brand cartons of Chenin Blanc he found in the bargain bin of the Sea Point Pick n Pay, off-flow from the best vineyards.

He loved the sunshine, and the rainstorms, and taking the Golden Arrow bus through the Hex River Valley, where a DC9 rusted in the middle of a wine farm. He adored the Cedarberg, dressed in the leopard skin of its brush, where he went hiking on his bad knees in badly tightened khaki shorts. He admired the silver trees standing sentry at Devil's Peak, the strutting and mumbling penguins at Boulders Beach, and the visiting whales in False Bay snorting as they lay on their long white warty sides.

Because he named them, these things were Solly's empire, the common subjects of his transport poems, as much as the rust-ridden Toyotas and Tata trucks and buses. Solly had a sense for the most complicated and ravishing perceptions which he built into the lines of his transport poetry, just as if he were catching the electric charge in a piece of amber. I couldn't imagine who would want to kill a man who generated this pleasurable electricity.

Everybody had gone. The cemetery clerk was the only person left at the grave. He had further instructions to complete. He read out some pages of Rumi and Hafiz in Persian, and then the same poems in Portuguese translation to an audience of one.

I recognised the lines as among Solly's favourites. Several of the Hafiz poems had been printed on what looked like a toy scroll out of a Lucky Packet. It hung above the battered Defy oven in

Solly's kitchen. In the months of June, July, and August, when the house was too cold to be comfortable, Solly read aloud forever from Hafiz while sitting in a chair and enjoying the heat of the oven. He didn't know how many hours he went on because the only clock in the house had only one idea in its head. The oven timer was broken and had been in the same condition since I'd first entered Solly's kitchen. Its red-and-white hands pointed permanently at forty-one.

Solly Greenfields's kitchen ... Solly se kombuis ... during my year of internship that kitchen near Main Road in Woodstock had been a second home. I could find my way through it easily and knew where everything was located, opening the sugar to chase away the skinny, knock-kneed ants, and finding the dusty bag of lentils underneath the sink without kneeling down to look. As interns, for those twelve months, taxi poets were not supposed to accept cash or credit from any quarter.

As interns, we wrote free of charge for anybody who required a transport poem, be they rich or poor, driver or passenger, suburbanite, or the occupant of a Slovo house. Before matriculating, we were supposed to be independent of any particular group, institution, or perspective, unaffiliated with a taxi company, or a railroad, or a school-bus service, or a shipping concern, or whatever.

As an intern I lived on hospitality. The greater portion came from Solly Greenfields. Solly looked after me, bought my Tegretol at a good price from Lunat's Chemist around the corner, and, in general, kept me occupied in his kitchen, talking hour after hour, while his tough brown feet soaked in a tray of Vicks-scented water and Marmalade relentlessly clawed the couch as if there was something to find inside it.

If it was really miserable outside, pouring cats and dogs as it did in July, Solly would run a bath at some point during my visit, bending over the taps and complaining as he opened them, and worrying out loud about the condition of the geyser. It was in poor shape but continued to produce as much hot water as he required. He continued conversing with me from the warmth of the tub.

In between Marmalade's advances, and with the help of hundreds of lines memorised from Amichai, Akhmatova, Brodsky, Andre Biely, Walcott, Whitman, Solly showed me that you hold a taxi poem by the wrist and take its pulse at the end of every line. He was never as interested in relating his own compositions, although those were the same taxi poems which invariably made me see a new fact about the world or maybe some old thing anew ...

My cat has the small brains of a dog,
And brings the smell of Nugget brown shoe polish.
When he shifts balance on the sill to observe the pastel hadedah,
He is a Hi-Ace which is the only thing gleaming
On Boxing Day
On the long road to Bhisho.

I should be honest and declare that the money Solly handed over to Lunat to fix my account touched me more than the actual lessons. He was constantly behind on his property rates. Taxi poetry made no millionaires. But to make up for it, as Solly told me, we had cash voices, like the announcers on Cape Talk who spoke so gaudily. They had money in their voices. If you listened too nearly to the ringing of coins, he said, you lost the ability to attend to the other noises in the universe.

Solly lived on the equivalent of a working man's salary, just above the financial level of a sliding man. The city's foremost taxi poet, its leading light, didn't have a bank account or retirement plan. He skimped on the electricity tickets he bought once a fortnight from Clicks. On a cold day he would pull out the plug behind the refrigerator, even take out the toaster and the television plugs, and claim that he could hear the credits ticking away on the electric meter on the wall, which he couldn't because it was digital.

The main subject Solly complained about, besides electricity, was his teeth, which caused him a good deal of subtle pain and sometimes made it hurtful to talk for fear of putting any pressure on the nerve endings. He had them attended to by a country dentist whenever he made it up to the agricultural town of Clanwilliam, by the Cedarberg, paying for fillings as he could afford. The dentist was an old friend from school who never actually received a dentistry certificate, and, for anaesthetic, used expired canisters of laughing gas which the patient was expected to bring. He bought them from the government clinic and bargained for every one with the nurse.

Given his difficulties with money, Solly was extremely parsimonious and outstandingly generous at the same time. He kept candle stubs at the back of the drawer as if they were the bones of a saint, and worried about the price of haircuts and leather shoes and the cat food he bought in bulk from Makro and slopped into a briny dish which Marmalade examined without enthusiasm.

Solly clipped his coupons and vouchers out of the *Daily Voice* and stored them in the pages of his verse anthologies. He thought that the property rates were out of hand and believed that taxation violated his human rights, especially GST. There was a powerful strain in his character which told him never to let go of a coin voluntarily, because it was never going to return to you. This same character tendency was related, in a way I cannot define, to his desire never to let go of a word or a sensation which could be applied in a taxi poem.

So, sure, Solly Greenfields was tight with money. Nonetheless, what was his was mine, and anybody else's who came within the radius of his affection. If there chanced to be a fish in the frying pan when you rang the doorbell, Solly would bring you inside and sit you down. Then he went back to take the battery out of the electric bell, thus stopping the malfunctioning clapper which otherwise continued to sound.

Solly would put the battery on top of the oven when he returned, making sure that it wouldn't get lost in the excitement. I bought him a battery recharger for the bell but it was rarely used for fear of running down the electricity. A jug of Clifton came out of the fridge, as pale as lemonade, but grainy and too sweet like the powder it was mixed from. I didn't mind.

In the long run, I suppose, the rule about money taught us politics from the bottom looking up, which is the only way to look at the world. But if you asked me right at the end of the year what those twelve straight months of intern's poverty actually taught me, it was the value of a good meal.

My mouth watered to recall that succulent fish stew. Solly's kos was the pride of the house, the centre of its heart, more important than the raggedy furniture he shepherded in from the pavement and the Woodstock dump, and maybe as significant as the big hardcover editions of Yehuda Amichai, and Rilke, and Eugène Marais, and perhaps on a par with the cat itself.

Solly sang the praises of the Cape snoek as he skinned and chopped it. The heap of carbon-blue skin grew on the chopping board. The fish released its not discomforting scent, almost like an expired jar of olives, as he talked.

"First and foremost, snoek—species *thyrsitesatun*, a member in good standing of the *Gempylidae* family—is the fish of the oppressed and the dispossessed, of whom we have more than a few on this continent. Your and my friend Karl Marx told us we must always think historically, thus to avoid the traps and illusions perpetrated by the ruling classes. So let us think historically."

Solly retied his apron, and sprinkled the naked fish with lots of salt and pepper. Marmalade, or perhaps one of those predecessors whose names I cannot recall, was aroused by the dense scent of the fish. He sprang onto the counter, attended to the fish's tail with velvet-button eyes. Solly shoved him off to the side, behind the butter dish, and continued his discourse.

"Therefore, historically, snoek has been the daily fare of the workers, and of the slaves brought here by the Dutch from Batavia, and of the blacks from the Eastern Cape, as far as Transkei, and of orphans, farm labourers, bus drivers, street walkers—and also of taxi poets. I am persuaded that our literary traditions owe a considerable debt to this insignificant fish. Isn't that correct? Am I speaking sense?"

"I agree. I've heard this lecture before."

"And you agree, Ravens. You give out compliments, Ravens. You find the common ground. That's a habit you need to unlearn, Ravens, because where the truth is, and where the middle is, are two very different places. Now that I am giving you two cents of advice, I'll make it four cents at no extra charge. Considering where you came from, you have a great head for ideas and concepts and speculations, which is a thing that will stop you progressing in the field of taxi poetry. Ideas, arguments, commonalities, every-day politeness—throw them to the birds. If, that is, you want to contribute something genuine. I also have something positive to say about the practice of composition. It's similar to cooking in terms of taking care of the details, much more like cooking, for example, than higher-grade mathematics, which I failed in matric. No, the functioning of your skull has very little to do with it. The best things come straight out of your fingers."

Here Solly dropped the thorny white pieces of fish into the bubbling orange tide of the stew. The pot began to crackle at the bottom. It was hot in front of the oven despite the electric fan on the table. The air was filled with so much raw pepper I wanted to sneeze.

I watched Solly as closely as the cat. I watched his fingers as they ran along the spice rack, picked up tubes and bottles, and brought a pinch of their contents to his nose, as fluently as if he was an organist at the Anglican cathedral. I wanted to remember the recipe for later, and his very words, every last one of them, in case one day I had interns of my own.

I wasn't sure when to add the tomatoes, how to clean the fish, what temperature to cook at, whether to add white vinegar and in what measure. However, I had been reading up on the subject at the public library behind Main Road in Woodstock. I had information of my own. I imagined Solly would be interested.

"Do you know, Solly, that during the Second World War, when there was a submarine blockade, they canned the snoek right over here, in Cape Town harbour? From there they shipped it over to the United Kingdom. So, for the British, in their minds it's associated with deprivation. Which explains its unpopularity over there, similar to sardines, which the British also cannot tolerate, but which the Brazilians apparently go crazy for. Plus and all, we have our snoek when it's just been pulled out of the ocean. It can't be the same when you are getting it out of a tin can. Or do you think so?"

Solly didn't answer my question. I waited a minute. Still no response. He kept stirring the stew and arranging the pieces of fish as if he was doing a puzzle at the bottom of the pot. He adjusted the timer on the stove although it had been broken since I first set eyes on it and would always be broken thereafter. Next he put his hand under the cat's claws, taking his usual pleasure in their sharp and bony print. The fierceness of his cats, one after the other, was his true joy in life. They could take on big dogs, and had a fighting reputation in all the yards down to the corner café.

I don't think Solly processed that I was asking a question. Maybe the pot was crackling too loudly in his ears. He had Gandalf's ears. They were populated by long white hairs which looked as stiff as the bristles on a toothbrush. He refused to trim them, although there were nail scissors on the basin in the bathroom.

Solly was defiant about his appearance and, in fact, it would have taken more to make a prepossessing picture out of the man than merely the subtraction of a few long hairs from his ears. I think he wasn't sure what he'd be left with if he started removing parts of himself for beauty's sake. He could have gone down to nothing except for his soul.

These stiff white hairs guarded Solly's mind, and they did a pretty good job. Sometimes it was impossible to sneak a full sentence past them and into Solly's consciousness.

Maybe men didn't have such good hearing when it came to the sound of my voice. They maybe didn't work on the same frequencies. Maybe they had the same hairs Solly did. Maybe they simply powered down their hearing when it wasn't in use. Whereas, in my experience, more women kept their ears switched on.

I didn't resent Solly Greenfields on account of his deafness. You could say that it was a professional hazard. Being a transport poet, and belonging as he did to the era of socialism and revolution and decolonisation, Solly spent years listening to bicycle horns squeaking like mice in township alleyways, to vintage trains booming like elephants in Kinshasa, to Casspir infantry fighting vehicles going to war along the Caprivi Strip and through the Chobe River, and tugboats cawing in Richards Bay against the freighters. That generation went everywhere, travelled on every conceivable means of transportation, and brought back the sounds of every wheel and engine and rusty axle.

So, I figured, Solly was entitled to be a little hard of hearing. He still had the trains and tugboats and bicycles ringing in his very furry ears.

When he dished out the stew, Solly went back to the subject.

"As I say, this is real working-class fare we're having tonight. So I am delighted you chose today to put in an appearance. Otherwise I would have been dining alone with the cat."

"To be honest," I said, "I've never had snoek like this. I thought workers liked fast food instead, like Bob's Burgers, or even a beirute sandwich, if it isn't the standard Gatsby. I have a problem with popular taste. When they have money to spend, on payday, they ignore the good local stuff which isn't mass produced and mass marketed. But you say we don't have the luxury to criticise the working class."

Solly dispensed a spoon of the stew into my bowl with each sentence, whether mine or his. Then he replaced the pot on the stove top. He slapped the glasses down on the table and poured water into them. I began drinking the soup. The pepper grains went straight into my throat.

On the red rubber mat in front of the oven sprawled Marmalade's prototype, hardly chastened, ignoring us and gazing up at the oven with avarice.

"For six or so, something like that, per kilo, we have snoek. And it's nourished all the poets, white, brown, black, yellow, and purple. Nevertheless, if you look at a span of centuries since the arrival of the Dutch on these shores, not one particle of recognition has this species received. If I am not mistaken, and I don't believe so because I have an excellent memory for such matters, there is not a single line referencing the snoek in all of our literature. It has been utterly erased from our history. And maybe,

Adam Ravens, you can fix that. When you matriculate in a few months you can compose a sonnet in honour of the snoek. Make me proud, kitten."

I wasn't sure if Solly was joking about this or anything else. He had something resembling a sense of humour, I suppose, which came out in conversation but it had to do with his whole attitude to the universe rather than any feeling for comedy on his part. Indeed, people regarded him as a forbidding figure, especially in the transport sector, and especially when it was related to the workings of the Road Safety Council.

You had to be righteous about the road situation, if you wanted, say, to lighten the butcher's bill over the Easter and Christmas long holidays, which ran into the thousands, as the long-distance taxis collided at speed on rural roads in the early hours of the morning. At the same time, Solly wasn't averse to a good joke, and maybe he even preferred a bad joke.

So you didn't exactly know when he wasn't being serious. It was difficult figuring his tone, even for someone who had been around him for many years. He had the same friendly, high-pitched voice as a lot of the men around the Cape, at least those who aren't the colour of a bed sheet. You couldn't be sure if his voice was rising because, maybe, he was pulling you back and forth on his line. Maybe that was just how his voice sounded.

Solly's taxi poetry had the same sweet-and-sour character. That was what made it special. It was volatile. You put it on one part of your tongue and it was as sweet as rock sugar. Then you shoved it to another part of your tongue. Suddenly your mouth was sour as a lemon drop, or bitter as kale.

I said, "Snoek, as such, I don't necessarily like. Too many bones, Solly. They're tiny, and there are millions of them. I keep having to suck them out of my teeth. Not once have I had really good, I mean excellent, snoek at Corky's, or those other fish-and-chips restaurants people talk about—Kalky's, Shorty's, and whatever. They put too much breading and too much butter, expecting that to make up for the shortcomings in the kitchen. In my opinion, you have the real secret to making snoek. What is it? I thought I tasted ginger in my spoon. Did you add it when I wasn't looking?"

I had almost finished. There was only a small amount of liquid left in my bowl. Solly buttered a slice of bread and handed it to me to mop up with. He took one himself and applied himself to the stew.

Solly seemed to inhale the bowl at the first taste, as if he was taking Vicks into his chest from the same plastic tub where he liked to soak his feet. He looked satisfied with his production. With his free hand he gathered the cat onto his lap and pressed him to his stomach.

After a minute he said, "You are quite correct. There is a small amount of ginger. I won't give you the recipe because you will only learn it properly when you prepare it for yourself, and make mistakes, and correct them. The clues I give you, however, are the following—remember the ginger, don't forget the capers, and finally, five minutes before the end, use more butter than my friend Herman the doctor thinks is reasonable. Although Herman is a country dentist, and not even a proper dentist, and, considering I buy it for him, he isn't generous with his anaesthetic. He only calls himself a doctor in his dreams. Which doesn't change the fact. You know, for most doctors nowadays, even being alive is unreasonable."

"Solly, I can't imagine you listening to a doctor's instructions. You don't listen to anybody, not even Parker, and Rooknodien himself, who actually was a doctor whose stethoscope you wrote about but whose advice you ignored. When are you then going to listen to Herman?"

A frown set itself on my instructor's face, as if he was deliberately dog-earing a page. "I don't need you to tune me, and give me stories, but you must never flatter me either. Unnecessary compliments are the best way to murder a taxi poet. Please don't butter me up."

Solly's idea was also part of the code. A good taxi poet strove to be accurate, fair-minded to all comers and claimers, and not to put on paper the first thing which came into his head. Everybody, no matter how humble, should get a place and a name and some shred of his story retold in terms of his contribution, however miniscule, to taxi history.

Where the companies expected their employees to follow instructions to the letter, someone like Solly Greenfields was more likely to follow the letters, which had a way of always leading him further than he expected to go and in fact up to the creation of the Road Safety Council. That was what precipitated the break with the Taxi Owners Association.

People said the relationship between the taxi companies and the transport poets was unique to the region. But it was never simple to negotiate, for either side. In my case the charm of a foolship in Parker's service had evaporated, I think for both parties, leaving between us the residue of some indefinable, but undeniable poison. I even had the sense, at Solly's funeral, that I, as a mere taxi poet, had stung Parker, who owned a taxi company. But how was it possible?

One last word about Solly Greenfields and me. Usually two people worked the inside of a minibus taxi—the driver, of course, and secondly the sliding-door man.

On a Golden Arrow bus, the second man would be called a bus conductor, or a gaardjie, or a sliding-door operator, and sat on a folding chair at the front of the vehicle. However, on a Toyota

Hi-Ace, or a Tata Vishnu, barrelling down Claremont Main Road or from Langa into the city centre, he was a sliding-door man and was therefore the central figure in our transport culture.

The sliding-door man, as defined by his name, reached back to open and close the long white side door whenever the van stopped, even sometimes when it was on the move and a passenger wanted to jump off. This sliding man incarnated the very spirit of the taxi, living and often dying in it, conceiving his children in the back and bringing them up by barking at them on his cellphone in the front.

He took all his meals on the run. On the front bench, beside the driver's seat, was, more often than not, a Russian or a polony-and-chips Gatsby doused in vinegar and heavy peri-peri sauce, with the pink rounds of polony, or the scarred pink sides of the Vienna sausage, showing out of the bun.

A Gatsby was not all that stood between a sliding-door man and a typical driver. They belonged to different social groups. A driver was not much more than a failed schoolboy, a Grade 9 who had been in the same class for five years, or a matric student who finally dropped out, and, with our economy in the shape it was in, had no other employment prospects. He counted as unskilled labour and was employed on an informal agreement renewed from one morning to the next.

The driver kept an eye on the tyre pressure, the oil, the engine, blockages on the motorway, and insisted that the radio was permanently tuned to Cape Talk 101 or one of the Clubland channels which played variations on house, or types of drum and bass, which my son Zebulon followed with scientific intensity.

Taxi drivers came and went, almost without names. They drifted from company to company, ran off to Johannesburg or Dar es Salaam with nothing but the lucky charm that they hung on the mirror when they turned up in the morning. After an accident they got carted off to the emergency ward at Groote Schuur and from there to the pathologist. You could work with a driver one day, never see him again, and never think twice about it. Their dice and rabbits' feet brought nothing, in the end, but the usual misfortune.

On the other hand, the sliding-door man, who harangued the passengers and brought in the pedestrians, spoke slangily as if he was always chewing gum. He dressed in loud colours and big lapels from Discount Warehouse. He would defy the world to keep the volume at number 11. He had far greater responsibilities than the driver. A taxi company rose and fell on the strength of its sliding-door men.

A sliding man possessed the talent for math, taking in and giving out the exact amount of change from his palm while the van careened from side to side. He did the arithmetic in his head and didn't make mistakes. The passengers took unkindly to getting short change.

Meantime, as he doled out the coins, he kept a grave watch on the cash bag. He was on the alert for medical emergencies, and dealt with troublesome fares like religious converters, schizophrenics on the loose from the psychiatric hospital, and pickpockets who sat on the rearmost bench and snaked their hands into the wallets of his passengers and who, if caught in the act, were liable to be thrown out of the moving vehicle.

A sliding man kept his cool. Unlike the autistic driver, he had a talent for networking and getting on with other people. Everybody was his china, his mate, his main connection, his brother, his bra. He talked his way past the roadblocks when the minibus was stopped and searched, and paid cold-drink money to the sergeants from a brown envelope which he clutched like a purse. Where relevant to his work, he maintained a good relationship with the local Congress Party structures.

Sliding-door men were notoriously persuasive. You didn't entrust your lady friend to the company of a sliding-door man. People said a sliding-door man could sweet talk any woman in a matter of minutes and bend her to his will—be she a schoolgirl, cherry, poppie, tannie, grandmother—and, for that matter, almost any man.

In sum the sliding-door man was a central agent in the transportation sector. He was a chimera, part politician, part social worker, part navigator and banker, nurse, and first responder.

On occasion, if you looked into one of the two-dozen or so Toyota Hi-Aces and Tata Vishnus fielded by the typical company, you found a taxi poet along for the ride.

The taxi poet recorded the shifting history of the taxi company, its minibuses, taxi bosses, drivers, and sliding-door men, and all the shifting sensations, impressions, and moving feelings of the participants, even those which were so subtle and ever changing that nobody besides a taxi poet could return them to memory.

These taxi verses were stencilled onto the side of the Hi-Ace or Vishnu. Parker still used the garage outside his house in Belthorn Estate for the purpose. He owned an electrical sprayer which heated and activated the paint as it spattered. In twenty minutes flat, even in my time with the company, they could inscribe the entire surface of a minibus. And it was, you know, beautiful. When you saw a Hi-Ace just as it emerged from the paintshop, she reminded you of an Indian bride who had mehndi done on her arms.

The hierarchy inside a company was never entirely fossilised. Once in a blue moon a driver graduated to the position of sliding-door man. About as often, a sliding-door man underwent a change of vocation, learned the basics of syllabification and versification, and took a position as resident transport poet in one of the companies.

Now as far as I am aware, I was the only individual in the history of the transport sector to transition from driver, at sixteen, to taxi poet at the tenderfoot age of twenty-nine.

I am not claiming to be special. I never felt I had any special talent, above everybody else, to be a taxi poet. What I had was good fortune. Solly Greenfields took an interest in my development.

Solly found me when I was still a driver. It feels like one of his golden clichés, if not a golden coincidence, to say that Walt Whitman brought us together, but it happens to be the truth. One day Solly boarded the Hi-Ace I was driving—Salt River to Parliament side—and discovered my keeping a tatty yellow-papered library copy of *Leaves of Grass* open on the seat while waiting for the light to change on Victoria Road. He recited the lines about lilacs and dooryards, as if we were exchanging the sign of secret brotherhood. Solly's middle-aged and grassy and half-purple face seemed like a garden gone to seed. There was something in it which made you trust him immediately.

I am sure that, for professional reasons, Walt Whitman was every bit as fickle as Solly Greenfields. Even about transport poetry, Solly could change his mind and then change it back, calculating and recalculating the relative validity of Geromian and Tsvetaeva, Virgil, Walcott, Emily Dickinson, and Robert Frost. Solly subtracted them from the list, his canon of golden writing, and then put them back and still grumbled about everything they hadn't understood and the narrowness of their concerns and the problems with their politics and the limitations of their style and removed them again and then restored them to their original standing. He went back and forth about most things, about Trotsky, Bukharin, Descartes, Léopold Senghor, Sékou Touré. But not for one minute was he indifferent to Whitman.

Solly never left me alone after that meeting on Victoria Road. It was he who encouraged me to learn the ropes as a sliding-door man. At that time, predating the formation of the Road Safety

Council, Solly had some degree of pull with the taxi companies. He spoke to Montalban, Parker's lieutenant, then to Parker himself, on my behalf, and tested me from a CNA question-and-answer booklet before I went for my standard-grade certificate.

Much later, after I qualified as a sliding-door operator, Solly instructed me in everything from the character of the semicolon to the construction of scenes in the extended narrative poem. He introduced me to the Portuguese-language classics, including Camões and Fernando Pessoa from Durban. He corrected my spelling, and let me type out my drafts on his electric typewriter, which had to be removed from its original packaging and replaced in the same box, cords and all, when I was done, the keys of which he cleaned with Glassex.

If it hadn't been for Solly Greenfields, in other words, I would still be at the awkward helm of one of Parker's Toyotas, drinking Iron Brew by the litre, living on polony-and-chutney Gatsbys from Golden Dish and Ottery Farm Stall, watching half-price Wednesday movies at the shopping centre while trying to see three shows on the same ticket, queuing in the evening to get inside the doors of Galaxy where both the Muslims and the Christians went dancing, and arriving at Wembley Road House at two o'clock on Sunday morning for hot dogs and frulatis but principally to keep my appointment with the goddess of meaninglessness.

Overseas, yes, it was a different situation. A fellowship at Oxford or Kyoto University led to a stint as the poet of an airline, shipping line, railway company, or a fleet of hydrogen-powered trucks and buses. Transport poetry was global, and by nature a technological-political enterprise.

During the Cold War, for instance, Charlotte Monaghan, probably the most respected poet on the world scene, moved from Belfast in Ireland to Groton, Connecticut, to work at the Electric

Boat Company, which manufactured atomic missile submarines. She had unique experiences which she sewed into her work:

In the torpedo tube I find an octopus curled in a nylon net,
Heady with salt,
Holding eight hands with my glove now,
Like the lover who gave me my sea-legs.

Charlotte Monaghan mentored a generation of underwater poets at Groton, waking up their waterlogged senses, teaching them her rough syllables. Monaghan's former students had shown the world something new and unprecedented about the bottom of the ocean. In recent years it seemed that every prize under the sun, as well as under the water, had gone to one of Monaghan's products.

Groton proved that education could work, that the right touch, in the right place, at the right minute, and under the influence of the right star and radiation, created secondary vibrations in a secondary soul. Monaghan, as a woman, had this effect. Maybe, as people who were lesser stars in the constellations of taxi poetry were heard to say, it was her only way of implanting her seed in another person.

If you couldn't make it to the established institutions, places like Rio University of Brazil, Groton was the place to be. If you had taxi poet dreams, Groton was where you might want to dream them. Even the city of Bangalore, in India, had a Hindi-language programme producing, in my opinion, rather good motor-scooter poets.

There was no parallel in Cape Town to India's traditions, which went back to the Sanskrit scriptures, or to the engineering prowess in Groton, which built enormous submarines and sent them beneath the Arctic ice cap, or to the Republic of Brazil's prestige and glamour. Our community was small in number, even if you counted parastatals like Transnet and the Golden Arrow Bus Service.

Plus, we made it worse. When we had someone valuable, like Solly Greenfields, we left him in poverty while we ran after Geromian's recent counterfeits of Brazilian-Portuguese literature. It was our condition: the most degraded elements satisfied our tastes while the best failed to arouse our senses. We left the roses and sunk our snouts into the trash instead.

This, in a roundabout way, was the motivation for my current job. I was as proud of it as anything I had once done for Parker. I had been appointed assistant director of the Jose da Silva Perreira Institute for Transport Poetry, based at the University of Cape Town.

I had never been to university myself and I was enjoying the opportunity to see how one operated, how the professors talked, how the old men and women were hooded for the graduation ceremony, and how the students whiled away their new lives on the steps of Jameson Hall and Rhodes Memorial where the stone lions kept watch.

The Perreira Institute was intended to raise the level of transport poetry throughout the region. It was a political objective, strongly supported by the ideological guardians of the Congress Party. In a new democracy—in a place which, before, had never cared to enlighten its people and, in fact, had kept them under the boot—increasing the standard of transport poetry was part of the revolutionary process.

Some argued that the money, the bulk of which was coming from outside the country, could be better spent on mobile clinics, secondary schools, and public works projects, like building roads and dams and solar collectors and telephone towers in the rural areas.

Others, including Solly and his polar opposite Geromian,

believed that taxi poetry could not be taught in a formal setting. According to them, road learning, not academic theory, was first and foremost. The discipline of taxi poetry must be passed from one practitioner to the next in secret, like Promethean fire. And yet, according to the same Solly, taxi poetry was also a song, a people's song of the fifty million, never intended to be arcane but to be sung on the Golden Arrow bus and the Hi-Ace and the commuter train, not to say in shopping centres and football stadiums and Wendy Huts, wherever a heart could be reached.

I wasn't so sure. But I wasn't sure of a whole lot when it came to causes and effects. Wasn't a cause as slippery to hold as a mermaid? In general, I was in over my head with my job. I had been feeling it particularly over the last couple of weeks leading up to Solly's death. I had the instincts of a taxi poet, or, at best, a sliding-door man, both of which were distinct from a good administrator's savvy. With red tape, my first thought was not slicing through it but tying additional knots and seeing how much weight I could hang on the end of it.

Because of my responsibilities at the Institute, I didn't have so much time for my own projects. For instance, I had never managed to complete the snoek poem which I had long since planned to present to Solly on his birthday. But which birthday?

One birthday had followed the next until it was too late. They had been stored away with the old moon. Since starting at the Institute I had tried my hand in a hundred different places, at committee meetings, and during sessions of the university senate.

In the end there must have been a hundred drafts of Solly's poem tattooed in HB pencil on the back of electricity company envelopes and inside the covers of Institute memos and budget documents, and in half the old books on my shelves. There were as many of them lying around as there were bones in a snoek and now not one would ever be perused by the man in whose kitchen I had grown up. None of them satisfied me. They stuck in my teeth just like tiny bones.

PROBLEM #2: Gerome Geromian. With Geromian, like my snoek poem, I don't even know where to begin.

Sometimes, composing a taxi poem, you pluck a thought out of you just like removing a thorn from your finger. Then there are times when you can't say where is the thorn and where is the finger and whether, in other people's eyes, your fingers might not have a thorny appearance.

Geromian had been mixed up in my existence almost as long as Solly, but in the way your life and your dreams and your language can be mixed up with a taxi poet you may never have met. To a young transport poet in Cape Town who happened to be me, Geromian's productions were just as significant as Solly's. There was something daring in him, maybe sinister, and smouldering like an old fire with sarcasm and coaly breath. Compared to Solly, Geromian and his works were far more glamorous and better publicised after he had been prosecuted for subversion. You were more likely to read a line of Geromian's on the side of a double-decker bus in Buenos Aires than anywhere in Cape Town: "The dancing road—uncoils—in the—ear."

When Geromian's taxi writings were printed inside the country, they bore a semaphore of long black dashes, page after page, where the censor for the old government intervened to prevent publication, objecting to a phrase here, an image there, or excising a reference to a notorious police shooting, an obscenity, or quotation from the proscribed works of Bukharin. The short and long, short and long and short dashes made you more determined to read between the lines.

Later, on Gorée Island, Geromian incorporated the censor's dash into his compositions. He claimed that there was no more beautiful line possible in a transport poem than the dash. There was no more beautiful and impossible word than the one you couldn't read.

Their work, Solly's and Gerome's, had begun circulating at about the same time, the early 1970s and the period of decolonisation, although in quite different venues. Geromian's taxi poems were licensed by the Brazilian companies, reprinted in the established São Paolo and Paris journals, and soon enshrined in the standard Academy of Brazil Press editions, the ones with the gold-leaf lettering on the side and beautiful scarlet cloth bookmarks cut in an arrowhead that stuck in the head of any young taxi poet.

The black dashes had become part of the repertoire of visual artists from São Paulo to Sydney, a code in which within the width of a Koki was encrypted tyranny and politics and taxi poetry, freedom of imagination, and the fantastic hopes of travellers everywhere.

In São Paulo, Manaus, Berlin, they knew about Geromian. Whereas Solly Greenfields' compositions could be seen either on the side of Parker's taxis or perused in mimeographed copies, stapled at the top and bottom, and available in Observatory, Mitchell's Plain, and Paarl, from the usual Trotskyite and left-Bukharinite libraries and the Book Lounge, assorted community centres, and trade-union halls. But it was not the proper context, as any professional said, to approach a taxi poem between a pair of book covers. It had to be seen in its natural habitat on the side of a Hi-Ace moving down a main route into Cape Town.

At any rate, Solly said, from the comfort of his bathtub, he didn't need universal distribution. If anything, the reverse was good. What was important was that his productions were accessible to someone who chose to track them down and made an effort. His readers should be as dedicated as he was. I wasn't sure I believed him.

Where Solly Greenfields was nearby, in ways too numerous to particularise, Geromian was distant. He was emotionally detached, especially when he was being friendly, as if he was leaning down to smile in your face, as he had done on the morning of my graduation ceremony when I qualified as a taxi poet.

Geromian was the speaker at the matriculation ceremony held inside Ottery Community Centre, next to the technical school which admitted me on Solly's recommendation at the age of twenty-one. Parker and Solly were in the audience, while Geromian was in the sky. Years before the Casturias Prize brought him global renown, and around the time of the feud with Charlotte Monaghan, whom he accused of plagiarising his work, he already had the style of a celebrity. He wore a linen suit and sandals, made the reporters bring him cigarettes, and only Silk Cuts would do. He was convinced that everybody, not just Monaghan, was plagiarising his work.

I got to talk to Geromian after the graduation, just for ten minutes under the awning as it poured cats and dogs again, but more cats than dogs. By Geromian I was dazzled, but repulsed, but nonetheless dazzled … but nevertheless repulsed and appalled. He was more down-to-earth than anybody in Cape Town, more salty tongued, more practical and cynical and openly lecherous about money and women, but at the same time, and in a way I couldn't quite resolve, he was also more cosmic than anybody, with an eye firmly on the day, in a hundred trillion years, when the entire universe would go dark and the proton at the centre of every atom would expire.

Geromian was also generous, after a fashion. Yet he didn't put a word in his speech about the contribution of Solly Greenfields. He had an individualistic perspective on taxi poetry. In this region, according to him, the taxi poetry movement was the creation of the individual, not the state, not civil society, not academic institutions and trade unions. The name of that individual was Geromian.

Language had something to do with their difference in popularity. Solly used the usual mixture of dialects, from minibus Fanagalo to tsotsitaal, including his own kitchen Dutch and high Cape Afrikaans. Geromian spoke beautiful Brazilian-Portuguese, up there with the most cultivated members of a Rio gymnasium. He wrote a good deal about sex, passion, and the female form. Recited in his accented Portuguese from a plinth, it exerted a pretty much soft-porn effect on members of the audience.

For nothing more than a boy from the Orange Free State, Gerome had a natural affinity with Brazilian-Portuguese culture—all its pretensions and continental grandeur, its uninhibited invocations of melancholy, soulfulness, cheap spirituality, and sensuality, from the fado, and Portuguese narcocorrido, to Ipanema Beach in December, black-bean stew taken with grated manioc, beheaded-coconut water absorbed through a straw, and those bikini models who rose and fell in the gossip pages, and the perfect geometry of the capital Brasília as seen from an aeroplane.

Solly would have lasted five minutes on Ipanema Beach if he had ever been invited, and he would have spat out his coconut water, and he would have claimed there was nothing in the whole immensity of Brazil, from Salvador de Bahia to the black water of the Amazon, to compare with what he had within five minutes of his door in Woodstock. And Solly would have been totally wrong. And, in a way, in his way that I sympathised with, he would have been totally right.

Where Solly was a man of undistinguished appearance, Gerome Geromian was handsome, leonine, and became more so with age. Geromian had beautiful long hair, old-man's hair as silver as the moon, and a beauty spot at the corner of one eye. With his long square jaw and physical grace, not to say the expensive black turtle necks which were his trademark underneath the linen jacket, he reminded you of a Brazilian movie idol. He didn't mind doing the reminding either. He would tell you how little it mattered to him when people compared him to Tony Ramos and Antonio Carlos Jobim. Geromian would care, I was sure, if the comparisons weren't flying around. But they flew around him like bullets in Cape Town.

Solly had a sweaty brown dome of a head from which he mopped the perspiration with a thin cotton handkerchief. When he wasn't in his kitchen, where he was truly at home, Solly waddled along the road. If you saw him outside the house and came over to greet him, you got the sense that he was intent on ducking your attention. At Ottery Community Centre, where I met Geromian for the first time and cornered him under the awning, I was almost ashamed to own Solly as my acquaintance when he came up.

In his cheap nylon trousers Solly reminded me of the head-master of a government school and especially when he pulled out his handkerchief. You half expected him to pull his lunch out of his pocket in a Tupperware and eat it in front of you with a plastic knife and fork, while continuing to dab at his head if the temperature was anywhere north of twenty degrees Celsius. He wasn't a romantic figure.

No wonder Solly was obscure. Gerome Geromian could publish a list of the separate parts belonging to a Defy refrigerator, and the reviewers, everywhere you went, would hail it as a cool triumph. None of them noticed that Geromian had more or less stopped thinking, and feeling, a few decades before.

Plus, Solly's sexual leanings were all but indiscernible. It was like trying to pick up a radio signal from over the horizon with nothing but a tuning fork. He never made an issue of it. In my hearing, anyway, he never admired women on account of their beauty or made much of younger men on the same basis, although he was receptive to the ones with bright and sweet personalities who were receptive to him, which was as far as it went.

Whereas Geromian inserted himself into pretty much anything that moved and breathed and had an opening to accept him. In every conversation with the press, Geromian made a boast about his life as Don Juan. He was alternately mournful, proud, minutely sensuous, and even jealous and passionate about his women, but he ended up leaving each and every one of them. He justified his behaviour in the form of taxi poems:

My road—which is only the trunk road to Dar es Salaam
Takes me from the sea-water snail—on your belly
To a conch by the petrol pump—
On the unsanded beach of Dar es
Salaam.

In conclusion: where Solly reminded me of eating snoek, Geromian made me want to drink cyanide. It proved that the universe, even the portion restricted to taxi poetry, was fundamentally unjust.

Geromian was on his way from São Paulo, or Rio de Janeiro, or wherever he was hanging around. He had been chosen as the recipient of the Institute's inaugural Jose da Silva Perreira Award. I had lobbied for the prize to go to Solly. Instead, the committee, dazzled by his Brazilian connections and his numerous awards and appearances, chose Geromian.

People were blind when they didn't know their history. Modern transport poetry, in my view, was the product of the decolonisation era. Nor could it be delinked from the advent of affordable diesel engines. People travelled around in their tens of millions on Toyotas and Tatas. That was a huge difference from the situation when a trireme, or horse and buggy, was the possession of an elite and the poem of a trireme, or the poem of a horse and buggy, was an evening's entertainment in the household of a wealthy man.

The difference, I reckoned, was also cultural-spiritual. Compared with the anonymity of the various Sumerian and Greek antecedents, like reed-boat poems and the *Odyssey*, a modern transport poem had a particular name, face, and a particular soul stamped on its every manifestation. It was named and dated. It came from a particular time, place, and Toyota, and yet one could never say who was going to find it. It was a postcard with no ultimate destination.

But that was just my view. Other people saw the thing differently, in particular the literature department at the University of Cape Town, who would know better than I would.

Taxi poets were supposed to be fond of irony. So perhaps I should have been delighted about the following stroke of irony. It was my job, as an assistant director of the Jose da Silva Perreira Institute for Transport Poetry, to escort Geromian around Cape Town while he was here, to see to his daily needs, to keep him out of trouble, to get him to his appointments with the press and the public, and to tend to his cosmological sense of self.

Attending to Geromian was part of my job description, according to Helena Bechman, my line manager, and I wasn't the type to resign on a point of pride. I was bad enough at my job as it was. Pride would have only increased my inefficiency.

Yet it seemed like a deliberate insult to Solly's memory that on the day following his funeral, Geromian would be touching down at the airport and counting ten thousand cruzados into his São Paulo bank account, that Geromian should be putting on his mock turtleneck while we were opening a hole in the ground, and that Solly should have been murdered while Geromian was murdering the language. If you recalled Solly's sonnet sequence on the days of the week, a Monday was the day for a bad coincidence.

Solly's funeral and Geromian's imminent arrival was a textbook case of a Monday coincidence, if you didn't believe that God had a hand in history. It was as if Geromian had a hand in the murder of Solly Greenfields.

Not that the two men had any real connection to speak of, either in life or in literature. They moved in different circles. They knew each other's names, probably one another's faces, but, from all I heard, they never made much of a personal connection.

Not that Solly disparaged Geromian's writing, although he went through phases of not caring for it. Not that someone like Solly Greenfields—and there was nobody else like Solly—not that Solly would come to Geromian's attention except, perhaps, in an anthology here or there put out by the imprint of a left-leaning Mechanics Institute. Not that Solly had ever reminded me that I ignored him once, one morning outside the Ottery Community Centre, and for one minute, in favour of Geromian. Not that Geromian would notice if an anthology containing Solly's compositions came into his hands. The only substantive interest Geromian took in external phenomena, after all, was in comparing them to himself. Everything was either a version of himself, an approximation to himself, something which could provide some service to his self—or it was beneath his attention.

The spirits of these two taxi poets were fatally opposed. Solly Greenfields was the chunk of kryptonite to Gerome Geromian's Superman. But Solly was gone.

TUESDAY

~

AS I ARRIVED at the airport to collect Geromian I still had gravel
in my eyes from the funeral the day before. I had five minutes to
clean them and forget about Solly Greenfields. I couldn't have
done it if there were five days remaining.

Inside the foyer were taxi touts, Somalis and Congolese and
Zimbabweans, middle-aged men in tracksuits, who were unattached
to the Taxi Owners Association because of their outside origins and
had to work in secret. They whispered just as you came through
the doors and followed you for a minute until they gave up. In
less time, if you agreed, they would lead you to a Hi-Ace which
sat with its engine off behind the multistorey parking lot. They
seemed to have no clothing on underneath their tracksuits.

I went past them. Since I was last there, the airport had become
modern. There were flatscreen televisions in the shop windows
and digital tickers along the top which streamed red numbers and

letters. At the counter, in an old-fashioned gesture, a shop assistant turned a bottle into a bolt of wrapping paper and followed with a ruler and scissors.

When I spied Geromian at the carousel, through the doors which opened and closed as other passengers exited, I felt unsteady. I hadn't set eyes on him in years. I had my resentments towards his figure. None of his sins escaped me. I was a taxi poet and I didn't forget. It was my job not to forget and therefore I couldn't forgive.

Yet, from some other place in my heart, there was a lurch of joy to see his figure in front of the carousel as the suitcases bumped along the machinery. It was all the stronger for being an inexplicable pang, as if my problems were done with because of his arrival. His taxi poems had a similar effect of consolation.

Geromian saw me through the door and bustled out.

"My darling, tell me, where have you been hiding all this time? I thought I would see you as I came off the aeroplane."

I said, "I figured you would see me as you came out."

"You are a sight for sore eyes, my dearest. Now do come, please, back in, and help me with my luggage situation. I brought two pieces which, if it's my usual luck, are arriving in Timbuktu at this very minute. Someone in the Timbuktu security office is measuring my good suit to see if he can have it altered to his size. And it's the only good one I brought."

"I'm sure it won't fit. They have a different stature up there."

"When I go there I have the feeling that everybody dresses like me. Now I know why. That's just my luck."

Geromian had good luck, despite the fate of his suitcases, which was the fate of all suitcases, to go to Timbuktu and be ransacked. He looked well, a man who was the product of a large amount of good luck. He wore a short leather jacket which barely came to his hips, underneath it a dark-pink shirt, and slacks which seemed to have been pressed five minutes ago.

I noticed the stud of an earring, just about invisible in one ear and imagined him screwing it into place each morning, and feeling for the next-to-invisible nut on the other side. There was a crispness in the way he spoke and moved, not a quality you recalled in his taxi poetry, which could be as languorous as Cleopatra. So he was different in person to how he was on the page. For a minute, I couldn't put this difference into words. Half my feelings, more than half, were like irrational numbers and couldn't be put into writing.

"I told them at your so-called Perreira or Ferreira Institute that if they wanted to see hide or hair of me, then you, Adam Ravens, must handle my visit. That was the sum total of my conversation with that woman who runs the stupid place. She, by the way, is an absurdity. Don't think I haven't met her before. We're well acquainted. In fact, at that conjuncture in the 1980s, I couldn't get rid of her and her desire to hero-worship me."

I said, "You mean Helena Bechman, our director. Yes, she often gives people the impression that they owe something in return for her attention. She has made it my job to see that you get everywhere safely and on time this week, and that the lecture on Thursday goes well. She's very concerned about it. Your reputation as a rock-and-roll type precedes you."

"We won't talk any more about that, thank you. There is one of my bags, which has delightfully returned from Timbuktu. You can just put it on the trolley, if you don't mind."

I wrestled the suitcase off the carousel. Geromian could have better managed his own bag onto the trolley. He had a solid frame, a barrel chest and barrel body and a boxer's nose. His nose looked as if it had been broken and broken again in the same bare-knuckle contests conducted on the backs of Tanzanian trucks, immortalised in the early-period transport poems.

If boxers did the impossible, got old gracefully and kept the wits they didn't possess in the first place, you might have mistaken

Geromian for a retired boxer. Not only did he look as if he had boxing in his past, he also had the personality for it. You were always in the ring in his presence. And he kept his arms up, never giving you an opening to retaliate.

"Ravens! The remarkable Adam Ravens! How long has it really been? Five years? Longer than that? When was I last on the continent however? Memory is no longer my servant, as she was in my younger days when she would fetch me all her finery. You know there is not much anymore to bring me this side. I have moved on, my dear. Things are different between this culture and I. I am not at all nostalgic, mind you. It's the privilege of a taxi poet to count the changes in things, isn't it?"

"Yes, I believe so. But also to remember what they were and, as well, to see how they really are."

He said, "Later, I want to hear more of your reaction to this news about Solly Greenfields. I heard it just as I was leaving São Paulo. I am sure you have something to say on that score. I will rely entirely on the validity of your opinions while I am here."

"I was at Solly's funeral yesterday in Parow. I feel that everything is different now."

"Really? Didn't we expect something like this to happen?"

After fifteen minutes at the carousel the second suitcase hadn't arrived from Timbuktu. Geromian went to report the situation at the luggage desk and see which country it might have been delivered to. I pushed the trolley alongside him and read the flight stickers plastered on the sides: Jakarta, Singapore, Salvador de Bahia. Solly, on the rare occasions he left the city, travelled up to a bed and breakfast in the Hex River Valley with only a cardboard suitcase, and the dentist's nitrous oxide, and the different pains in his every different tooth for company, and his over-manicured cat in a cage, and cans of brown baked beans for his subsistence. Now where was Solly and where was Geromian?

Geromian knew his advantages over us. Even in the airport I saw he already made a judgement concerning my evolution, and it wasn't a positive one. I was the kind of person who had lost his second suitcase. I was the kind of person, if not the exact same person, who would wear his second suit around Timbuktu even if the legs were too long for me and the blazer too tight on the belly. The way Geromian looked at you might even bring back the memory that, under the old government, his father had been a judge in the rural areas when it was common to dispense a sentence of flogging or hanging.

And if you were looked at in this way by Geromian, you might be disposed to argue, in your defence, that his grey-blue eyes were too clear and too close together and that when they stayed on you, and you happened to have eyes which were closer to the shade of hazel, then it seemed that there was no bottom to them and no proof that anybody was at home.

Who was I to be the judge, or to pretend to be the judge? As Parker's driver, my main claim to fame was collecting speeding tickets along the length of Main Road and never attending traffic court. Where was I and where was Geromian? His friends and associates and closest enemies included, to mention only two, the Sultan of Brunei and Charlotte Monaghan in Groton. And Charlotte he accused of plagiarising his material.

So he could be the judge, or the judge's son. I didn't have the same desire to send people away.

I hadn't told Helena Bechman how I was bringing Geromian back. It happened to be in a Hi-Ace, not a private car which was five times the price. I was as economical as Solly taught me to be.

So it was a minor act of defiance to take a taxi. Helena wanted our visitor handled as tenderly as a Fabergé egg. She should have chosen another person who didn't contemplate treating Geromian like Humpty Dumpty instead, and pushing him over the wall.

The minibus was empty apart from us. I sat next to Geromian on the back bench. He didn't complain, although I expected him to. It was one of Parker's taxis, by no means luxurious, but serviceable, if your idea of good service is losing your hearing.

The sliding-door man was impatient to collect the change. Sliding men were like that, men in a hurry and ready to make the world miserable if it would save fifteen seconds of their time.

As he returned to his seat, two more passengers arrived, and then three more, guards in their airport uniforms, and then five more workers when we paused at the far end of the terminal, and a very fat young man who had fought his suitcase into the taxi. He sat near us, on the opposite side of the taxi, and wheezed and rolled up the sleeves of his shirt and had an unexpected expression of satisfaction on his large face, as if he was a fat saint who had been sent to taxi world to redeem our sins.

Geromian looked just as happy as the saint. Maybe I didn't have to worry about putting our visitor in a Hi-Ace. Maybe I made the right decision by bringing him back in contact with transportation. This same type of vehicle, and far worse, had been his working environment on the road in Zambia and the Belgian Congo, as the Cape Town taxis were Solly's habitat. I could close my eyes and almost forget that it had been three decades since, as a young master in the field, this particular Geromian composed one transport poem after the other, each of which was worthy of respect for its fierceness and its astonishing angle of attack, and the jagged edges of its lines which could almost make a paper cut on your fingers. The Cleopatra mood, slow and sensuous and self-absorbed, arrived later.

The minibus sped down the fast lane, overtaking trucks and Golden Arrow buses with their orange-and-green livery and even a horse and cart toiling along the road, the cargo of building materials on the back partially concealed by a blanket and ropes. There weren't so many working horses in the city proper but just as you got out of town you would start to see animals in harness. One would be feeding on the green siding between two spread-out blocks of flats, its fringed brown shoulders flexing as it enquired into the grass, and another would be standing doubtfully beside a rusted-out petrol pump.

There was a lot for a horse to doubt. Behind the short embankment were acres and acres of tin roofs. The makeshift buildings went back from the motorway in both directions. Alongside the shackland were chessboards of cement Slovo houses, poured in their thousands by private construction companies. The buildings were already connected by telephone and electric wires.

It was a new settlement, and hadn't been there when I was a driver. Much of it, apart from the Slovo houses, appeared all at once along the road. One day there was only scrubland and scarecrows, which turned out to be electricity pylons. Then the next day, when you drove through, there was a community of tens of thousands in place, from Shangaans who came from the northern provinces, and Sothos from the highlands, to Xhosas and Fingos and Pondos.

At the cooling towers the minibus abruptly changed lanes and pulled up in the breakdown lane. The sliding-door man called out the window to nobody I could see.

More passengers appeared, four in all, swinging over the concrete divider from nowhere with their possessions in plastic bags. They were duly packed onto the three benches, two more with us, until even the fat young gentleman who was in reality a saint from above began, under his labouring breath, to sound dissatisfied.

I counted the taxi's twenty-three occupants. That same haze arose which might have been onions or might have been tobacco or the murmur of the tongues in forty-six shoes.

Geromian wasn't a person to take lightly. At the Mount Nelson, in accordance with the instructions their famous guest faxed in advance of arrival, they had installed an ioniser machine and a Brita filter on the tap and were busy removing electrically charged particles from his room. They had made sure to buy the special brand of blackcurrant tea he required. Helena and I had delivered the bed sheets to them from the only linen shop on the continent which stocked quality material. I couldn't imagine how the same man once slept on the bed of a truck proceeding down Zaire Route 1. It wasn't the Silk Road and it couldn't have been much of a bed. The silk in those sheets would have been worth more than a Bedford truck.

So I was nervous about the news of this first adventure returning to Helena Bechman, who, unlike Solly Greenfields, heard everything in earshot and followed it up and was like a bloodhound if you happened to make a mistake or filled in a form in taxi poet's style, which might even mean taking the questions more seriously than intended. To cover up my suspicion of what Helena was going to say, and distract Geromian from all the passengers, I began to talk again.

"Can I speak honestly? I don't understand your hesitation about accepting the award from the Perreira Institute. You shouldn't be ungrateful for the recognition, Gerome. There are other members of the profession, in this very city, who would give their eye teeth to be chosen as the recipient. Someone like Solly never got the recognition."

"Ah, what other people think doesn't interest me. Their validation is not required, for which I thank my lucky star. Didn't Solly get the benefit of a clear conscience? It's getting rather full in this taxi, isn't it? It reminds me of something. On Zaire Route 1, shortly after Lumumba's death, I went on a flatbed Bedford truck with ninety-four others, politicals. We drove three days nonstop to escape the gendarmerie. Let me tell you, your Helena Bechman frightens me more than any gendarme of the counter-revolution. I was on the point of telling her that any such institute is worse than useless, that it is a useless and fraudulent exercise, and, at base, illegitimate. That is what I desired to tell your friend Helena."

"And you didn't because?"

"I am not nostalgic but I have interests here. Suppose I wasn't averse, my dear, to the chance to look you in the face. I could never tell how your story would turn out. You and Solly were at different stages, one at the beginning and the other at the end of his useful life. Yet you were like two peas in a pod. You even began to speak like him. You still do. Like many other people I would have said you were like a son to Solly. It was only later that I realised you have the habit of being a son to many fathers."

"Oh, Gerome, I was never near as good, or fit to be compared to that man. Apart from the quality of his work, he had a heart which made me feel mean. It didn't begin and end with taxi poetry for Solly. What he was proudest about had nothing to do with himself. It was the Road Safety Council and the promise of upliftment to the community."

Despite myself, I kept talking. Since Solly Greenfields had passed I'd had nobody to relate to. Solly, despite the hairs in his ears, had listened to my stories around town. I had spent years travelling around the municipality, from the flooded tin shacks in Gugulethu to the rose-walled Italian-style villas in Durbanville, collecting taxi-poetry material. It was as interesting a cross section, in my opinion, as anything you could find in Rio or Salvador de Bahia.

Solly opened his hairy ears when I had new information to report. It could be something as simple as a sensation, like the apricot-jam windows of the Salt and Pepper towers at five p.m., or the mottled purple hands of the proprietor at the back of the Mowbray corner café which happened to look the same as the snowballs he sold from a glassed-in cupboard where they could never breathe and neither could the several flies on the inside of the glass. Solly showed me how to incorporate such a simple perception into a line, or he would do it himself and present it to me in the form of a taxi sonnet, taxi villanelle, taxi sestina, or, on the rarest of occasions, a taxi ghazal which would fly into your mouth on wings as delicate as a butterfly.

After a minute Geromian returned to the conversation.

"I was surprised to hear of Solly's death because he survived so many years without watching his words too carefully. Somehow, through all of his conversions, to Buddhism and Hinduism and left-Trotskyism and right-Trotskyism and then back to Judaism and Jainism and Tolstoyanism, he managed not to alienate his backers in the transportation sector, not to say the Congress Party. Certainly he would criticise the Congress Party although someone could ask the question of whether he was too invested in its history to see the magnitude of the decline. Now, to shoot him down? What has it come to, the revolution, and all our dreams of a new culture which I had a hand in creating? They lose every second suitcase, as regularly as clockwork. Now to assassinate a taxi poet?"

"Nobody said it was an assassination," I said. "I am not even sure who had a reason to kill him. This is a place where anything can happen, which is the reason for taxi poetry."

"It's basic logic about Solly. One bullet, I grant you, means that suicide is still a possibility. If there are two bullets in the man, then, if it is suicide, it is a case of exceptional resolve. After six bullets, well, my angel, my thoughts are turning in the direction of murder."

"I don't know if there were exactly six bullets involved. It was a figure of speech, you understand. There were probably only five. I don't know if one bullet makes a difference."

"It makes a difference if it's coming in your direction."

Geromian looked around, because there was no room to turn his head inside the minibus, and saw the acres of tin roofs, and the sand roads between them, and the shacks pressed against the concrete barriers of the highway. It seemed that this shackland went on forever, over the hills and dales, and that it was forever increasing. It was as old as the hills and dales themselves and as new as yesterday when somebody had been nailing four cardboard walls to a plastic sheet for a roof. The sight must have brought something back to my companion.

"I don't know about your so-called turns of speech, Adam. If it's a spade, I call it a spade, even if today's typical taxi poet would compare it to a pen or a hoe. I never believed that taxi poetry was just about speaking cleverly and stretching comparisons to the point of absurdity."

"There I agree with you."

"Ah, but with all the respect, I am not sure that you do. In my case the straightforward attitude belongs to the core of who I am. I grew up in the old Orange Free State, under the old power structure, in Clarens and later Jagersfontein, before they threw me out on my ear. Assuming you belonged to that structure, then everyone was on the same level. There was no pretence allowed, apart from owning a Mercedes to go into town in style and shop at the Greenacres. So whatever faults existed on the political side, and you can hardly accuse me of ducking them, we spoke plainly, as you can see in my taxi poetry. If, as you say, butter cup, six bullets were fired, then we would call it an assassination. Therefore, there were higher powers involved."

"I truly cannot say. Solly had a big heart, and a tough hide. When he began in his career, he needed to be the toughest just to survive, to say nothing about the upheaval after the formation of the Road Safety Council. Except that it's a jump from there to outright assassination. Will you do something for me? I truly don't want to sit here and split hairs with you concerning Solly's death. It's too painful."

Geromian didn't reply at once. Maybe it wasn't a good sign that I bulldozed him into silence at the back of the minibus. Maybe it wasn't good for me to be in his company, and maybe I shouldn't be allowed around anybody except Solly and Zeb.

Around Geromian, or somebody like Helena Bechman, or even Parker, I was going to win every conversation. Sometimes it would be overt and they would agree with my assessment of how the argument went. More often, I would be conscious of secretly winning the exchange. So many secret victories would conspire to ruin my character.

Who was I to win? The previous generation behaved as if they had been born in chain mail. They needed to fight at the political level, against the Special Branch who banned them, and placed them under house arrest, and raided the taxis, and also against the quietist churches and mosques, and against the conservatives in the universities, and against the radicals who argued that transport literature was an unaffordable luxury just so long as there was poverty and torture and oppression, which would be until the end of history, when nobody would be in a need of a taxi poem.

On Helena's instruction, I had followed up with the hotel and made sure the ionising device was properly installed. I offered to take Geromian around, arrange appointments with old acquaintances and supporters, to go with him to the old places where taxi poetry had been brought into the world. So far he wasn't nostalgic to do anything. He had transcended Cape Town.

So it was a surprise to learn something about Geromian, that the country town of Clarens was still the focus of his memories, and also of his conversation. The later taxi poetry cast a gauzy light on it—its church politics and churchy wives and their factions, Clarens peach brandy, which when you poured it in a tumbler had the colour of honey, and the balcony society and the bundling on an evening when a girl's body, under her clothes, was as hot and fresh as just-baked bread, and the lines of share croppers at the pay table on Fridays, and all its partridges and pear trees, and famous milk tarts which were covered with a square of material from a torn shirt, and canvas-backed Bedford trucks once deployed against Rommel.

In Geromian's taxi poetry, which one was encouraged to treat as autobiography, the community of Clarens was dominated by the figure of his father, a magistrate under the old government. By the standards of the time the father was an enlightened man and a moderniser. Nonetheless, he jailed labourers for travelling with a torn pass, seized the property of poor people when it was coveted by his friends, and covered up incidents of agricultural abuse up to the level of farmers' killing their labourers.

I felt that Geromian the son resurrected the father in his taxi poems, only to exorcise the spectre in the same gesture. Just how much juice could you get from having an old man who persecuted other human beings? What did Geromian want? A medal?

Someone else could be the judge of this issue. They could be the judges, Geromian the father and the son, the magistrate and the taxi poet, since they were so handsome.

Geromian's good looks were noticed by everybody and associated with his writing. Whereas I had no real appreciation for male beauty, except Zebulon's. He surprised me, as a child, by always being a creature of exceptional beauty and possessing the most beautiful arms and hands and beautiful wild expressions and having the most amazing laugh. The tones of his voice were very pure, like something you coaxed out of a piano if you were a proper musician. Up until Zeb I didn't dream that a boy should be the most beautiful being on earth. Afterwards, the fact was obvious.

Having forgotten about Solly, Geromian was interested in the shanties. But it was only as a chance to condemn.

"What's new? Just this spreading poverty and desperation. The basic relations of power have never been altered. Congress, which is supposed to be the voice of the people, permits the people to live in poverty, knowing the police will keep them down in case they rise up. It's a question of exchanging one form of the police state for another. Capital is always protected."

"Actually they are busy upgrading this part of the location."

"This is supposed to be an improvement?"

I said, "I believe so. From how people used to live."

"I know how they used to live. That's why we called for a revolution."

Geromian wouldn't know it from the motorway, but all those wires, strung between the ramshackle buildings, proved that the government was something different from a taxi company. In the course of the previous decade, whatever its failures, the Congress Party had succeeded in electrifying the informal settlements.

In exchange, the residents of the townships and settlements, in their tens and hundreds of thousands, voted candidates from the Congress Party into office every two years. The friends of the Party built the coal-fired power stations and put up the transmission grid and took their share of the international loans which came in to pay for construction.

It was a taxi poet's bargain, between the Congress Party and the people—power, in the form of electrons, in return for power in the form of Parliamentary seats.

The job of a taxi poet, or former taxi poet, was never done. Attending to Geromian didn't count for the whole of my Tuesday. After I dropped him at the hotel I still had work up at the university. Teaching was underway.

There were three separate classes at the Perreira Institute. In their first semester our students studied the history of travellers' and transit and wanderers' poetry. They went from Sumerian reed-boat poems and the *Odyssey* through to the present, which includes figures like Ismail Babangida on the Nigerian railroad, Florenzio on the merchant navy, modernists like Auerbach who, as a connoisseur of extreme conditions, went down to the seabed in a bathysphere and up to the top of the atmosphere in a ramjet in pursuit of new sensations, not to mention the subway poets known only by the initials on their graffiti.

July through October was the practical session. The Institute organised daily workshops, small so they could be effective. The students met with Judy, or Gil Etteh if he was in Cape Town. They composed transport poems and dealt with subject matter as diverse as trucks and container ships and rickshaws pulled along the Golden Mile by men in animal-skin waistcoats, which had the richest smell. So what I learned in Solly Greenfields' kitchen, and on the Hi-Ace Super-T belonging to Parker, the students at the Institute developed in the context of a seminar room.

University types argued that transport poetry went back to trireme Pindarics, if not to the Homeric Catalogue of Ships, and, perhaps also, the undeciphered inscriptions on ritual and calendar boats. There had been a tendency in recent years to declare that there could be no such thing as culture, or history, without transport poetry. But that didn't mean you had to have an institute to have taxi poetry.

Solly gave me his unsparing criticism concerning the hubris of setting up an institute in Cape Town, which had to do with the idea of the Institute, and also the folly of situating it in a place where the Muses were indifferent. Nonetheless, there was an energy and electricity circulating around the Institute which created sparks both good and bad. I heard that in Gil's workshop, where the participants were encouraged to attack one another, the feuds between the factions were no less bitter than between rival taxi companies. But this was also true of the city factions, down the mountain, who, like scholars, never relented on a grudge or estimated an opponent higher than his very weakest line.

In their sessions with Judy or Gil the students learned the basics. They counted beats and syllables, collected interesting rhymes which would go into their compositional stock for life, arranged verse paragraphs, and figured out how they wanted the text to be inscribed on the panels of a Hi-Ace, whether it should be loose or spare, jagged or nicely balanced. Above all, they saw that each good line of transit poetry must be stretched to its ideal length and pinned there. Then it vibrated properly. There had been a move to introduce the most demanding forms into the second-semester workshop, especially the difficult-to-master Mozambican villanelle.

The most important things, of course, couldn't be taught or summarised, but had to be felt in the heart and in the breath and in the way one travelling thought or perception caused you pain while another gave you pleasure, and one taxi poet made you seasick, as if you couldn't stand up, but the other opened out your mind, line by line and fold by fold, like origami.

I ran the third-semester course. It was the practical component. The students were placed in internships with the various taxi companies. Some went to Parker, as I once had. More adventurous interns went to Madlala, Moloto, or Rosenstein's motor enterprises.

Female students, who were almost a third of the class, went disproportionately to Mrs Rooknodien. They tended to believe they would be more comfortable with a woman, although it didn't always work out. You could have good luck or bad luck with someone like Maya Rooknodien. And, in general, I didn't think there was any rule to enjoy a successful internship. It was a process of trial and error, sufficient time on motorways and minibuses, by which an intern found a place in the profession.

If you were wise you wouldn't say a word about luck to Helena Bechman, founding director of the Perreira Institute, who was sometimes my idol, and sometimes, which weren't necessarily different times, the bane of my existence. I couldn't tell her that Solly had been unlucky to be murdered. Helena had been trained as a scholar in transportation studies and had a plan for every contingency, including life itself. She didn't believe in luck, unless it was her bad luck that I was still on her faculty and that she was the first person I ran into.

I never got to say an unnecessary word in Helena's presence. When it was me, I noticed, she went straight to the point and wouldn't be diverted from it, whether it had to do with a budget I hadn't entered into a spreadsheet or the placement programme, which sent the students into taxi world and sometimes to work at the offices of the Road Safety Council. She didn't stoop to pleasantries around me.

Under different circumstances, when she wasn't on duty, she could be a fiercely friendly redhead, a flamingly friendly redhead, someone who sucked the oxygen out of the room. Her friendliness, and her academic charisma, was almost like a form of hostility. As she talked to you she touched you on the arm and her paper-lantern face glowed with benevolent feeling. She handed out the most sincere but excessive compliments, as if she could only discern the good side of your being. For a minute, until she turned somewhere else, you might as well be the centre of the universe.

For some months Helena had turned away from me. She was strictly business. This was maybe because she believed I was in love with her, which was not the exact truth, and maybe because she worried that, absent her firm lead, I would just tie the conversation in knots as always.

"You got Gerome to the hotel? No complications I should know about?"

"He's at the Mount Nelson in the room he wanted, which overlooks the Planet Bar. I had to terrorise the manager into providing it, and to buy the oxidisation or electronification machine Gerome mentioned in his fax. At least it's the Ferreira family paying directly. Thank goodness for these rich Portuguese. We can't afford it out of our budget."

"Perreira, not Ferreira, like the Institute. Ferreira's the tennis player. Above all I don't want complications. You are a great one for creating complications."

"This week? I wouldn't dream of it."

Helena looked at me a little more closely, as if she was going to find something she hadn't found before. She wasn't going to. We were stuck in a loop which kept us going around each other.

To my shame I was crying again in her presence. Helena wore so much make-up that I worried I was going to sneeze at the powder and offend her. So I held it in. I frowned. I put my hands in the drawer of my desk. However my eyes watered at the sides.

As a result, because I wept slowly on this occasion as before, Helena believed that I was in love with her. And, you know, she treated me gently. She knew that I was going through a difficult time. She even had a plan for my feelings.

She said, "I wanted to come to the funeral but Sebastian had some debacle with a visiting scholar and he felt it was appropriate for his wife to come along because patriarchy, it turns out, is not yet dead. Sebastian is a huge fan of Solly's work. He always says that taxi literature is the soul of the transport industry and that I am wasting my time on the linguistic aspects. You must be devastated."

"Absolutely. Absolutely, Helena. Plus we'll never know what went down. Given the situation with the taxi companies, it would be a miracle if we ever have an explanation of Solly's death. They are in collusion with the authorities. Maybe explanations aren't everything."

"Maybe not. In any event, even if I didn't know him as well as you did, I was an admirer. If you can't manage, let me know. I am here if you need."

"I'll keep it in mind. And give Sebastian my regards."

The Bechmans had a marriage made far from earth and, in fact, in the stratosphere where a regional taxi poet could never ascend, although Auerbach had made it there and Geromian had gone to the stars. Helena and Sebastian Bechman married while they were enrolled in the rigorous programme at the University of Lisbon, where even the students had heads which were as white as swans.

They were an unusual couple. Despite Sebastian's reputation, and despite the continued existence of patriarchy, it was at least debatable that, of the two of them, Helena was the brain and the real scholar. She was a taxi linguist, considered to be among the best in the world.

Taxi poets didn't necessarily get along with scholars of the transport sector. The two groups didn't share priorities and philosophies. They didn't find the same things interesting. Nonetheless I thought Helena's intellectual work was solid, not the product of some passing theoretical fashion. She had shown that the dialects used on networks of Hi-Aces and Microbuses drew, at the level of vocabulary for everyday objects and practices, from Nollywood and Bollywood, Fanagalo, Sesotho, Sepedi, and even Cockney but, at the deep level of grammar and syntax, much more from Portuguese and English. She had also shown that the language of taxi poetry was unrelated to the daily speech she recorded on the minibuses.

We were lucky to have her as director of the Perreira Institute or the Ferreira Institute or whatever the family's name was who gave the starting capital and who had known Helena's mother extremely well. Helena was a star in the academic sky, a red giant. There was nobody else as fierce, as flaming, as irreducible as Helena Bechman, and certainly nobody for whom I would so gladly shed tears. So I was generally glad to see her in my office.

It wasn't a social call. Helena had a real reason to pay me a visit and had been moving towards it.

"One last thing. Rumours have reached my ears about a possible student boycott this week. I believe the third-semester students are organising it. They may not attend Thursday's ceremony. I don't know the exact nature of their political objection. They have their utopian ideas about a revolution in the transport sector. A driver will be magically on the same level as a taxi poet and every dictator on the continent will simply vanish in a puff of smoke."

"The way things are, I can't imagine what the students have to criticise."

"Adam, a little straightforwardness wouldn't harm you in life. At any rate I can't fix all the problems in the world by waving a magic wand, not this week especially. What I can take care of is the reputation of this Institute for integrity. You, I hear, are on good terms with that Antonia girl in the third semester?"

"Antonia Chirindza, from Mocímboa da Praia? My favourite in that year. She's very interesting. You should ask her about the difference between here and Mozambique, how we could be on different continents as far as language is concerned."

"More often than not, when trouble is brewing on campus, she is the agitator. I am told the same is true again. Talk to her, if you can, with my blessing. See if you can have them call off the boycott. I don't have the patience to do it myself. It's so difficult to build something like the Perreira Institute and yet everybody is so quick to tear it down."

"Well, Helena, the students don't see it as their problem to build, but to make sure the foundations make sense to them."

"You have too much sympathy for them. Next year, when admissions come around, remind me that most of these would-be revolutionaries are first-language Portuguese. And to whom are they teaching a lesson? Sebastian and I belonged to the Party, as disciples of Toure and Basil Carlos Bernstein, decades before these kids came to political consciousness. It may not be apparent but I date to the days when petrol was still cheap. We meant what we said about revolution."

You could tell her historical period from Helena Bechman's personality, if not from her reddish freckles and red politics. She had the sparky, whirring, clutch-changing spirit of a petrol engine. Her motor was always on.

Helena was right about the Portuguese speakers like Antónia. They spoke the world language which had been dominant for decades, and not only in the field of transport poetry but in politics and culture and economics. In the Portuguese dictionary our students found the proper words to challenge authority. Brazil might be the world culture, the centre of classical values and a continent in its own right, but it was also the source of the most radical doctrines that you could find in the Portuguese language.

The Mozambicans also absorbed the revolutionary consciousness of Frelimo, Frente de Libertação de Moçambique, which ruled the country through the regional transportation structures, despite losing the last election. Historians said that the regional transport culture was, in part, a result of the 1974 Revolution of Carnations. Could taxi poetry have been conceived without the example of Pessoa, without an intimate acquaintance with Alvarenga Peixoto, without Aguinaldo Fonseca and Fonz?

I said, "The students have their own impetus, Helena. The transport sector is not what it was when we were doing our internships and fellowships. The students have new battles to fight. One of their struggles has to be against us. Otherwise they wouldn't be taxi poets in the first place."

"It's because you believe this nonsense that I trust you to deal with this."

"Then I am happy to serve."

And I was promptly left alone to serve. It was one reason I hadn't been fired yet. I was the only faculty member who had once been a driver, and then a sliding-door man, and then a taxi poet.

The others didn't have that experience. Judy had made her career out of teaching taxi poetry despite hardly travelling on taxis, and talked about minibuses of the mind and conceptual routes rather than the physical thing. The same applied to Gil Etteh. Gil, who was so refined about the subtleties of a taxi poem, was boorish and deaf about the true values and teachings of taxi poetry. It proved taxi poetry had no necessarily positive impact on the individual. A soul such as Gil's was too well defended to be pierced by a punctuation mark.

Yet, in the view of people like the Bechmans and the administration of the university, they were the model staff members. I was the problem, supposedly. And I probably was. I felt Helena was just waiting for something to go wrong with Geromian, and then to portray it as my fault. She didn't necessarily want me working at her Institute. When she told me about my failures I always had an answer. It was a mistake to have an answer, as these situations went, but far better than not having an answer.

The untenable nature of my position was obvious. I was no good as an administrator. I could never balance a spreadsheet. The dark rumours of a disciplinary proceeding seemed more real since the time, against regulations, I took a third-term seminar to Grand West, on the Golden Arrow bus from Claremont, and forced them to listen to different people and their different

74

hearts and tongues that could change as quickly as the symbols on a lottery machine on the thinly carpeted floor of the casino. I loaned the students copies of Bukharin and Walt Whitman which they read when they should have been doing the preparation for Gil or Judy's courses. I even encouraged them to loaf, to lounge around on minibuses, to follow moonbeams to wherever they landed, and to close their ears to Gil's ten commandments for the composition of a transport poem.

I got away with nothing. In every case, the news reached Helena Bechman's ears. Thereafter she made her displeasure known to me.

Sometimes I suspected that Helena had kept me on only because it would be unnecessarily cruel to fire an individual who wept out of the love of you. Surely Helena Bechman had better people to weep for her?

The Jose da Silva Perreira Institute for Transport Poetry, where Solly refused to set foot, consisted of four red-brick buildings situated high on the east slope of Table Mountain, just below Rhodes Memorial and the stands of pines which you saw from the motorway.

The garage was the largest structure on the grounds. In it we housed a motley fleet—the Hi-Ace which leaked Valvoline, a dented Volkswagen Microbus, and some motorcycles. It wouldn't be mistaken for the University of Brazil programme, which operated a hovercraft, or Charlotte Monaghan's diving bells, which took her classes to the bottom of the ocean. But it was a start. Maybe it would end nowhere and maybe we would end up on the moon.

I found Antonia Chirindza in the workshop. She was sitting on a short chair next to the Microbus, a thick welder's mask over her face, with sparks flying everywhere from the welding machine.

Next to the machine she was unexpectedly delicate. I hadn't seen that subtle quality in her before. I had always been too impressed with her poise and perfect manners, which struck me as typically Mozambican, at least from a certain social class. She had a good reputation as a mechanic on the Volkswagen, one of the rare female students who did. I imagined that was also a product of her childhood among depots and workshops in the truck town of Mocímboa da Praia.

Antonia saw me through the sparks. I greeted her while waiting for the yellow-and-blue shooting stars to singe my skin. She seemed to have been expecting me, although I doubted Helena had given her a warning since they didn't communicate. I watched as Antonia shut down the machine and was reminded of Parker's mechanic. Sometimes I thought that we at the Institute were preparing a new generation of taxi poets, our young sparks, for a world which didn't exist anymore. Meanwhile we neglected to teach them about the actual behaviour of the companies.

Helena Bechman was not wrong to send me as her negotiator. It was one of her better plans. I liked Antonia, and even identified with her. She was my favourite student in that class on the basis of her intelligence and command of all the forms of taxi poetry. Her gift was for the unsuspected line which stayed unsuspected even after you heard it from her lips. She took lines from Shona or Matabele and made them new. For example,

Love, my touring sister-in-law, has to be fried
like a mealie-cob in the pan of courtship,
sides reddening from the incessant turning
from the front seat of the Toyota to the one who sits in the back.

Antonia had far better prospects than me. Her career in the transport sector could be remarkable, if only she made a good beginning, and always pushed at the possibilities of the language, and thereby expanded the borders of her own thinking. Someone like Antonia was infinitely more solid and also more daring and more confident than me at a similar stage. It might have been because of her family's money, and connections, in Mozambique, and her education at an elite escola particular. It might rather have been some quality in her soul which warmed you, if you were close enough, like a piece of coal burning in the fireplace.

So everybody, except Helena, adored Antonia. I wasn't sure that I was in love with her but it wasn't beyond the realm of possibility that Zeb was.

She said, "Can I ask you first, what is this all about?"

"Take your time locking up. I just wanted to have a word, and, if possible, ask you a favour."

"Whatever it is. Only I can't take back the past."

"I don't expect you to do that."

Antonia wasn't a simpleton. She knew the admiration in which she was held by the faculty and the other students. You could tell by the way she moved around, almost like a cat that was metering and yoking in each of her movements, even if it was the garage and nobody was necessarily watching. She was always on duty as Antonia. Her accent would have done a Carioca proud in the noblest gymnasium of Rio de Janeiro.

She wasn't a student one could be cynical about, someone whose consciousness-limits a teacher could immediately identify. Personally, I was altogether disarmed by Antonia. I didn't even mind her political tendencies, which were more demanding than the choice I had to make, along with Solly, between Trotsky, on the left hand, and Bukharin, on the other left hand.

Like Helena, to be sure, I didn't see why the students' first target was the Perreira Institute, and what plan they had to advance the cause of transport poetry after demolishing the premises, and what they would do to the transport sector once they had brought every Hi-Ace belonging to every taxi company to a complete stop.

The students didn't so much have ideas you could engage with. Instead they were in the grip of a general feeling that the world was out of joint, and they should set it right, but without knowing that it was as easy to make the world worse, by uncontrolled action, as to make it better.

Unlike Helena, I wasn't irritated by their vagueness and lack of pragmatism, and their desire to make things more complicated than they already were. I could never have admitted it to Helena, or Gil Etteh, because it would have confirmed their darker suspicions, but I preferred having such young taxi revolutionaries around, even if I was the thing which would have to be revolved, instead of the young careerists.

Even if Solly disputed the premise of any institution promising to inculcate taxi poetry, he agreed with my position inside of it. Solly had observed that the most revelatory experience, for a revolutionary, was living beyond the limits of his own revolution, and then to see the next one. Only then would you know if you were a true revolutionary, in your heart of hearts, or another species of conservative.

According to the same Solly, a true taxi poet was somehow on both sides at once, more revolutionary than the revolutionaries, more conservative than the conservatives. In my own case, I suspected, the terms were crossed. Antonia was the real thing.

I asked, "Seen Zebulon recently? I've been trying to track him down. He doesn't reply to my calls."

She looked as if she wanted to smile. Then she didn't. The fine, coffee-brown, stiff features in her face went even stiffer. There was something she didn't want to tell me and it was not unconnected with Zebulon.

"I haven't seen him in a couple of days. Try the Pepper Club.

You know it, right? Zeb prefers it there when he has something on his mind. It's not likely you'll see him at the Institute at this time. So what's the scandal, Adam? Can you tell me?"

"I'm his father, Antonia. I don't need an excuse to want to see my son. There's certainly no scandal."

Zebulon could be suspicious, as secretive and difficult to befriend as a cat, but I knew something about the geography of his life. He hung around with Antonia and that same revolutionary circle. They listened to similar bands and spent their evenings in the Long Street lounges.

Zeb, like someone I knew who once worked in Parker's company and learned from Solly Greenfields to correct a draft of a taxi poem as if he was breaking the bones in his own arm, was attracted to the foreigners. He collected them as his friends. Antonia was one. Her home in Mocímboa, in Mozambique's far north, was the refuelling spot for trucks on their way to Tanzania and points north.

I sympathised with Zeb's inclination. It wasn't only Antonia. Mozambicans who came to the Perreira Institute were the best of the best, the beneficiaries of the continent's best system of escolas particular. There were other students from closer to hand, like Rebecca Siweya from Polokwane, and Ronald Padayachee, for whom I had developed considerable affection. Somehow Antonia, who wasn't half as conscientious as Rebecca and didn't have a fraction of Ronald's lexical skills, and had never been as receptive to the wisdom I could have transmitted to her, was the one I adored.

And if you adored somebody, you worried about them. Antonia didn't look great today, as if she hadn't slept since the end of the previous week and had, instead, been poring over all the pages of Bukharin and Whitman like there was some message in there which nobody had noticed before. She seemed to be angry before I even asked my favour.

"I hear you are a ringleader in the boycott which is being planned for this week. It would be extremely embarrassing to the university. Helena Bechman has sent me down to reason with you. And I believe, for myself, that there is something worth protecting here in the Institute, whatever our faults. So I would like to be able to work out a deal."

"That's your favour?"

"It's what I'm asking from you, in exchange for whatever trust you think I have rightfully earned."

"Well, first of all, I reject the idea of a ringleader. Every one of us has a mind, and brings her own experiences to the collective. As a collective we sent a letter about the boycott to the administration. Up to now nobody bothered to take us seriously."

"I do."

"I accept that, because you are not always so loyal to the Perreira Institute. But, professor, there is no point having an intellectual conversation, and some pie-in-the-sky exchange of ideas, when money is all that's at stake. The Institute board has been running after the most retrograde elements in the transport sector. Meantime they get the legitimacy of being associated with our creativity as young taxi poets. Solly Greenfields, who you talk about as if he was a saint—he didn't want the Institute to fall completely under their sway."

I said, "You shouldn't be taking Solly's name like that. He believed in scholarships, which you people from Mozambique may not require, and he didn't mind if the money was coming from the Taxi Owners Association. In that way he was true to his own father."

With the mention of scholarships, and Solly's opinions, which I knew better than she ever would, I shut her up. I almost had a bad conscience about it. If I was also true to Solly's principles, I couldn't defend the ethics of the Institute. Under Helena Bechman's direction, going to work at the Institute felt like entering a modern taxi company instead of setting foot in Solly's kitchen. I wasn't about to persuade Antonia otherwise.

But it was my assignment to delay the boycott, not to find myself on the side of the students as I usually was.

I looked down at my boots. These boots were tough brown leather, from Manaus, and had lasted since my first day as a sliding-door man. I wore them when I suspected that the day ahead of me was going to be as tough as the leather.

These seven-league boots had taken me onto the side steps of a thousand Hi-Aces. They had taken me into Solly's kitchen and through his life and opinions and to the rim of his untiled bathtub and, just yesterday, to his funeral.

They were patient. They had waited beneath an unhappy bed every evening when I was with Zebulon's mother, and had faithfully attended me to the provincial hospital in town where Zeb had been born three weeks early and needed an incubator for ten days. He was the size of a frog, his chest the only thing you could see moving underneath the glass. The boots' heels were hardly worn down when I ran my hand along the soles.

I said, "Oh, Antonia, can I say something embarrassing? You remind me of myself, the deluxe version. I admire the revolutionary spirit in you, which wants to make a question out of every situation. At the same time, as a taxi poet, you have the opportunity to elevate thousands through your language, which is new life. As we said, language is a new life form on the planet. Don't take the first chance you have to tarnish the Perreira Institute. The dickens gets into you, in third semester. You used to be so young, and accepting. What did we do to you this side?"

"That's not a real question. Of all the staff, you were the one who told us to make a question out of everything."

"For me that's also a question, the question of questions. Maybe

I was flat wrong. I fear that we ruin you in the course of your education, take away your common sense, and instil the idea that all you need is to take extreme positions. After all, you look at the faculty, and how we go on against each other, and how can you, as an intern, think there is a different way? But, in the end, taxi poetry got started by people who made great sacrifices and compromises. Now, why are you too big and too grand to compromise?"

It was the longest speech of my life. I didn't know why I was uttering it, and why Antonia should be its object. I stood there glowering in my Manaus boots. But I was by six inches the shorter person.

At the same time, I was thinking that Antonia could be a good influence on Zeb. She was serious and he was a drifting mind. I would like that their friendship deepened and I didn't mind how much. But I didn't know that there was anything between them.

As an apprentice in the field, Antonia had a certain originality. Her early productions were curvaceous, from line to line, and filled with bright lust and satanic revolutionary pride. In person she wasn't so very fluent. She even stuttered, like a boy, when she wanted to say something about which she harboured an intense feeling. I hadn't seen her like this before.

"Sir, you said yourself that taxi poetry is about looking into things which other people won't, or don't, but which are completely obvious."

"So you have found what exactly that the rest of us ignored?"

"We believe that, through the taxi owners associations, the most reactionary forces are attempting to control the transport sector. It's a very different balance of forces here compared to Mozambique, much more reactionary. The space for imagination and critique is closing by the minute. We believe Geromian would stand with us, if he understood how his presence here will be used, and what it means to accept the award. For him, what does mere money mean?"

"I wouldn't be so sure of the virtue of taxi poets. Geromian's not necessarily what people think, some kind of model of revolutionary virtue. I was with him this morning. Being here, accepting the prize, he claims priority in the history of taxi poetry. I say nothing of the fact that, over here, he is fêted on every side as a god. Whereas I believe a taxi poet has no religion. And one of the gods I don't believe in is absolute and perfect justice. You can't fix everything first, from the taxi companies and monopolies and the Taxi Owners Association to the Congress Party and whatever. Else you will be consumed with justice and you will never put a line of taxi poetry on the back of a Hi-Ace."

"That reasoning makes no sense. You don't think a line of transport poetry should be judged depending on the longitude. You told us that on the first day of your seminar. Why should morality be any different? Why should we accept behaviour over here that wouldn't be tolerated in São Paulo?"

I could have gone on talking all day, although on some other topic than the boycott. But I saw that Antonia also wanted to escape. It put me out of sorts. I had a lot of knowledge, apart from taxi poetry, which I was prepared to share with a young woman with Antonia Chirindza's bearing. I could lavish everything on her that Zeb rejected.

I could see in Antonia's face that she would also reject it, and that, like Zebulon Ravens, she also had some place better to be than in my vicinity. I would never be loved by the interns at the Perreira Institute in the way I loved Solly. I would never even be loved in the way Geromian was loved or even Gil Etteh, who taught taxi literature without the benefit of a travelling soul. I couldn't say why I was undeserving of love although it didn't trouble me much.

I saw, counted out in Antonia's clever face, the exact monetary value of the career I had pursued since Solly Greenfields found me on Parker's Hi-Ace. It wasn't zero but it wasn't so very large either. The results were tiny compared to the input, like the sheer quantity of conscious existence which went into any line of a taxi poem.

"I don't even have the right to advise you as a taxi poet. I am merely a pettifogging fraud. I haven't written a syllable since October. What say I set up a meeting between you and Geromian? Convey your issues to him directly. And I'll make sure Helena Bechman reads your letter. If he disappoints you, if she also disappoints you, then you can call a second strike and I will fully support you. We can be together in disappointment. Can you take it back to the collective? See if you can postpone the strike?"

"I'll speak to them. Because of what you did for us by exposing us to the freedom of your opinions, I am prepared to take it back. But this is strictly a favour."

"I accept your favour, Antonia."

We shook hands. Even in my boots I was half a foot shorter than Antonia. I felt dissatisfied with the length of my limbs.

I said, "Glad we could solve it temporarily. I do suppose, if there's one place you expect to have a symbolic protest, it would be at an institute for taxi poetry."

It was the first time the idea occurred to me.

On my way home, since I was going past that section of town anyway if I took the wrong taxi at the Rondebosch rank, I went by the Pepper Club. The door was chained.

As it happened, one of the members of the Institute's first-semester class was also protesting. He was hanging around the Pepper Club building, sitting on the steps, and admiring his spindly long legs in the late sunshine.

This protester would have had many freckles, you couldn't help thinking, if his complexion had been any lighter. Despite his wanting to be as prickly to the touch as a porcupine, you saw that his face was too sweet to ever be convincingly sour.

This particular student wore shorts and a denim jacket. On the back of the jacket was printed a skull between whose bony teeth wound a python. The skull was raised, in relief, so you wanted to run your hands along its yellow temple and put your fingers through the black holes it had for eyes.

I didn't admire the jacket. For more than a year I had wanted to throw it in the bonfire, or give it away to a sliding-door man who was passing by and would remove it to the ends of the earth.

If I had any courage I would have disposed of the jacket in some way. For what this student had was utterly precious, and even temporary if he wasn't fortunate. He had his own beauty which you could see whenever he was concentrating and the effort made his face narrower. Maybe it wasn't as obvious as Antonia's and maybe I was so sensitive to it because of the funeral. Nonetheless, his beauty, which was physical as well as spiritual, was more convincing than anything I ever developed in a taxi poem.

This first-term student, with his dandelion eyebrows that were always about to blow away, had a very different cause to his comrades like Antonia, and wasn't so concerned about the concentration of power in the transport sector and the marginalisation of the taxi poetry movement. He happened to be protesting my existence.

PROBLEM #3: My son was more like his mother than I could tolerate.

Zeb was tall like his mother, six feet two inches at the age of nineteen and a half. If you didn't know any better he seemed just as innocent, or, rather, as innocent as she seemed. He had his mother's honey-brown eyes which, at moments of great emotional intensity, swirled round and round the pupils, just like kaleidoscopes. To see them swirl had some strange effect on my soul.

The last time I saw them swirl was two weeks ago, when, out of nowhere, Zeb decided to be a sliding-door operator and maybe not even complete his courses at the Institute. Otherwise, it was rare for me to detect anything more than a flash of feeling in Zeb. It was a point of honour for him to have no discernible emotional life around his father.

I had an idea, not just from Antonia, that I might run into Zeb outside the Pepper Club. Like any parent, however, I didn't necessarily admit to my ideas.

"Hello, Zebulon. This is a nice surprise. We haven't talked since when? Last Thursday afternoon, was it? I was just speaking to your friend Antonia up at the Institute. She's really become such a lovely woman. I had Solly's funeral to attend yesterday. How did your weekend go? You had all those plans."

Zeb looked at me suspiciously. "Nothing to report. Saturday night there was a DJ from Johannesburg at Utopia, whose show I couldn't miss. He's a seminal music thinker. Before that, I don't remember."

"You never remember anything."

"We went to a Chinese restaurant for Mom's birthday dinner. Her new boyfriend came along, the one who used to be in the wrestling team. Did you forget to call her for her birthday?"

I said, "I sent your mother a card. I didn't realise that the wrestler was still around. By now I thought she would have turned him in for a juggler, or someone who swallows fire maybe."

"Don't kid around. You always kid. And it's not a subject to kid around about. He's extremely strong. He can pick her up with one hand."

86

"So? It's not such a feat to pick up your mother, in my opinion. And, you know, that is pretty much what you expect from wrestlers. Antonia didn't come along to your Chinese dinner?"

He asked, "Why should she? She has better things to do. And she was busy at the Road Safety Council. You always mention her. You must be jealous. There's nothing going on for you to know about."

"I'm not jealous. I just want to understand your life. And Antonia is one of your few friends I can have an adult conversation with. Unlike most people her age, or at any age, she has depth. That's all I want to say on the subject."

Zeb stood up. There was still sunshine in this part of town, outside the Pepper Club on Long Street, where there were small hotels and backpackers' establishments, the Turkish baths, restaurants which advertised game dishes in the window, kudu and warthog which came with roasted potatoes and green beans, and a pastel mosque which had stood on the same lot for a century, and tuck shops run by sombre Somali men with their shelves of expired bread and batteries and boxes of fruit juice.

There was sunshine here. But it was Cape Town, and we could see slanting rain five hundred metres around the office blocks and bank buildings, where people were bowed beneath their umbrellas. Elsewhere, in Kalk Bay or Delft or Khayelitsha at this very minute, there would be storms, or summer floods which took away thousands of shanties, or rainbows, or frost.

I wasn't too concerned about the wrestler. I knew enough about my son not to trust the admiring way he talked to me about older men, and especially the ones who happened to be involved with his mother.

Regarding his mother, there was some pain in Zeb that I couldn't extract for him. Sometimes, like now, Zeb talked at some distance to his own words, as if his heart had been glazed like a ceramic pot. It was simply a strategy, I believed, an inexpensive defence against something residing in his mother.

Neither was I so innocent, some people would say, and one of them might be myself. I displayed no concern about the wrestler, which, in Zeb's mind, implied that I didn't care, in some way, about him. We did it to one another, Zebulon and I, and as a kind of compulsion. The pressure between us was insufficient, so that we had to push down on each other.

Just as it became unbearable Zeb laughed in the very same way as his mother did, and smiled at me as his mother once had, as if he was about to wince, and then changed his mind one hundred and eighty degrees. He didn't seem worried at all.

I changed the subject. "You're back early from campus. How's the job going? They treating you right?"

"If I hurry through the filing and scanning I just have to sit at the front desk and check people's cards as they come in. I've been reading a lot of early taxi poetry, which is the best. As far as the job goes, there's still time for it to go wrong. You can never tell."

Because Zeb was my son, he had precocious opinions about life and taxi poetry which were, nonetheless, much more informed than they sounded. I could tell because I had to deal with ill-informed opinions every day at work. He had taken a part-time job at the Perreira archive which was one of the units at the Institute. He worked there four afternoons a week, part of his financial-aid package. He had Friday off, not a difficult job. Besides, the money would come in handy when he wanted to go out in Clubland and hang around lounges and go to gigs where guitars were set ablaze. I couldn't necessarily afford to pay for all that.

I resented that the Institute charged full tuition for Zeb despite the fact that I was a member of staff. Helena Bechman hadn't wanted to change the policy, however. She thought it would encourage members of the faculty to have children. None of the good scholars at the University of Lisbon had large families.

I was on good terms with the head librarian at the Perreira archive. She had many hours to reflect on her disused sexuality and just as many hours to spare on good works, like watching over my nineteen-year-old son, and keeping him happy without knowing that his father was behind the whole idea.

Zebulon—this is what I heard—was good at his new job. He was popular with the staff, although quiet, and possessed of a soft and doubtful manner. He was also, as they said, good at computers and had become the unofficial priest of the IBM Junior stack and tape drive.

He was in charge of a section of the archive and was already learning the Dewey Decimal categories off by heart. He filed documents, scanned photographs and letters, labelled boxes, cut up and stored lengths of microfiche in the climate-controlled room in the basement. There were rare materials in the collection which they already trusted him to handle—San transcriptions and photographs of their cave paintings, primary materials relating to King Moshoeshoe and Dingaan and Paul Kruger and the Bleek-Lloyd archive, and other documents which recorded the early history of transportation. They were doing God's work.

What did God's work involve? They recorded transit poetry which would otherwise be turned into scrap metal. They photographed the old stately Golden Arrow buses as they were taken out of service, and had created an extensive collection recording old Microbuses and Hi-Aces before they were junked, and Transnet locomotives which had been inscribed along their flares, and motorcycle taxis and church vans.

The archive was a great place for Zeb. As a child he preferred to be by himself than with other children. He was busy and lonely at the same time, and could spend many hours bringing order to his kid's life—sorting out records and cassettes, alphabetising his books, repairing the carriages of his model-train set with careful applications of superglue. When I still lived in one room above the Steers in Plumstead where I could see the neon sign go on and off in the evenings, Zeb set out his toys in precise rows each time he came to visit and then packed them precisely into their wooden boxes when it was time to go again. But he liked to do the packing in front of me.

I still recalled Zeb's air of total absorption in his arranging activities. It defined his character. His very fine eyebrows sharpened around his head, which was itself covered in fine, straight brown hair. When Zeb had to pack up at my apartment, he started well before it was time to go because he wanted to do everything properly and in plenty of time, an attitude which must have been implanted in him by the moonshine on the evening of his delivery, because it didn't occur in either of his parents.

After Zeb finished his packing, he meticulously dusted off his knees and elbows and buttoned his jumper to the top. He was so careful about everything and assumed the world would also be careful with him. He stacked up his wooden boxes at the door and sat there cross-legged, waiting for his mother to turn up. This memory plucked at my heart, as if a hand was pulling at a guitar string, and some unexpected chord rang out of the cavity.

"Your mother told me you haven't been sleeping at home. You stayed away the entire weekend? A simple telephone call would suffice, to let her know where you are. Who were you with, Antonia?"

"Let me check my memory banks. Oh, sorry, I can't remember. Next time I'll tell her before she gets a chance to complain. Is that good enough for you?"

"Don't be vague with me, Zebulon. Would it kill you to sit down with me at some point and explain why, of all things, you've set your heart on becoming a sliding-door man?"

"I agreed to talk to you about it, yes. But I can't do it now. I have a lot going on in my life. You can't just pull in and expect me to have nothing going on. When I am ready to talk I'll call you."

"Zebulon, you only call me when you need someone to rescue you, or one of your connections, from some Clubland pickle. Other than that I never hear from you. I don't even know if I should think of Antonia as your girlfriend or not. I am ready to listen."

There was nothing I could do except keep talking and have him watch me through the glass in his soul which, as in a fairy tale, no sound I produced could ever penetrate. It was the thing I truly feared, much more than Parker and Montalban, or Geromian, and the student radicals, and the university administration, and their Congress Party brethren.

I mean, I feared my son's readiness to slide the door between us shut. Any sign of disagreement, and it was closed tight as a submarine hatch. I should sympathise with his desire to be a sliding-door operator. He had practised closing the door with me for what seemed like an eternity but may have been only as long as thirty months. I felt as if I had lost a child and gained a brilliant adversary. He was perspicacious about my faults and not unwilling to rehearse my debts for things left undone.

What my son did was inhuman, although I could scarcely blame him for it. He had learned his inhumanity, his readiness to slide the door shut, from the cradle onwards, thanks to his mother.

In my opinion, intolerance of dissent and contradiction, when it was as pronounced as in Zeb and his mother, made life, love, complexity impossible. Everything had to be just so, or the door would be closed in your face. I could never understand how I could be so guilty, in Zeb's eyes, in God's eyes, to receive such a punishment.

It hadn't always been so tough. When he was five years old, and even up to the age of eleven, Zeb would talk as directly as a person could, and straight at my head, as if he needed to be right in front of me. I couldn't leave him for a minute to jot down a note for a taxi poem. Everything I did interested him. During the day, he wasn't content to be anywhere else, in the kitchen, or in his bed, or with his model trains, if I was elsewhere or even if my attention was elsewhere. He wanted to do his collecting and archiving while I watched and did nothing else. So Zeb revolved around me every hour.

Just like his mother, the latest incarnation of Zebulon resisted me in a state of the eeriest calm. My son didn't get angry with me. He didn't have any strong feeling about what he was doing. He simply refused to comply, to agree, to negotiate with me, and even to reason in his own defence.

I didn't detect, in his face, any sign of movement in his heart. It was as if, in my presence, his heart refused to beat. And it was surprising, because he didn't have a stern expression. Zeb bore on his shoulders a face which was innocent in every detail, from his dotted eyebrows to the slight red freckles on his cheeks. To look at it again I felt, for no reason I can devise, that his insides were made of strawberry jam. I didn't like the idea of his being out in the city at the same time as Solly's murderer. It wasn't safe in Cape Town and never had been for a boy who wanted a real life.

"One last thing. I know you have your own money from the job and whatever is left from your scholarship. Does that imply I can't assist you?"

"I don't need money from you."

"I am absolutely not saying that you do. Where you are concerned, I am just a worrywart." I spoke too much, but I went on heedlessly. There was something about the situation of being a beggar-in-reverse that I liked. It was like trying to force a taxi poem on a reluctant spectator. "In case you need a taxi from Clubland. Put my mind at ease."

"If you insist, I'll take it. Do you mind taking something for me? Since I'm not going home right away I don't want to be carrying this package around. Can you take it for me?"

"I insist, in exchange for the peace of mind. But you must also pay me a visit, in return. I finally had the television put in. Come and watch the football if you want. Bring any friends that you like. Bring Antonia."

"Why do you mention her so often?"

"Because I know that you're close. But whoever it is, Zeb, it really doesn't matter. I just want to see you once in a blue moon. My point is, if you need anything, just come. You have the key."

I was given a brown-paper packet and handed over the envelope. It went directly into the pocket of Zeb's denim jacket, the one with the snakes and skeletons. It was a good deal of money. I winced at the idea of the envelope falling out in the middle of a taxi. The jacket he was wearing didn't have sensible pockets. If I criticised it Zeb would wear it forever on his thin shoulders.

I couldn't imagine why anyone could have bought such a jacket for my son, in all his beauty. Then, as if I was recovering a memory from another life, I recalled buying the thing myself for his last birthday. He had chosen it from a shop in town in which there were racks of such jackets and Ben Sherman shoes with their white treads, and a shop assistant with scarlet hair and scarlet patches on her lizard-like forearms, and a ring through her nose which made me want to lead her down the road and leave her there. I still had fears Zeb would bring her, or someone like her, back home.

I said, "So I'll see you around."

"Yes, see you around."

I put his packet in my backpack. By the time I closed it he had disappeared into one of the stores. For once I didn't mind the separation. I even felt, after leaving the Pepper Club, that I had achieved a kind of omnicompetence. I had his packet and he had my money. The thought brought a glow into my face. I could thank my boots for whatever victories I achieved today.

Further down, around the bank buildings, the rain had blown away and then the wind had blown away. In the other direction I could see the cable car being winched up the mountain, trembling on its long rope. At the furniture shop on the corner, the proprietor was bringing down the metal shutters and fitting the chain into the padlock. The sunshine was unusually dense for the middle of town, and even penetrating, so bright that it seemed to be forming a dream of everything around me, and I seemed to be alone in a blister.

Through the streets, from Parliament side, came a convoy of tall black vehicles, blue and red lights flashing through their black windshields. It would be a cabinet minister or a director general, someone selected from the higher echelons of the Congress Party, who was now trying to rule a place that never accepted being ruled.

I had some power of my own. I had found Zeb a job where I could keep track of him. I had survived Solly Greenfields, my mentor and morning star. I could even say that I had inherited his rights over Cape Town and its grand minibus culture and its elongated taxi ranks and its circuit-board streets. Nobody else besides Solly and I cared to make them sacred and find every detail of their manifestation interesting. I would do my best to justify Solly's bequest.

In Solly's work, as in a shell you picked up on the beach through which to audit the cosmos, you heard the fisherman voices of the sliding-door men, choked on the brassy engine fumes of a Hi-Ace, and hid in the back of the train to Mitchell's Plain as the brown sidings rattled back to town and the water towers and railway warehouses approached. That was a power more enduring than a director general.

94

Compared with all that, so what if my son slipped out of my hands as easily as a salmon? In return, I slipped into Zeb's hands and he would have to figure out what to do with me.

I believed there was one reason Zeb wanted to be a sliding-door man and that had to do with the effect on me. It was a criticism of everything I had done with my life since my time with Parker. I could remember, if I chose to, the everyday drudgery, from the routine curses you found in your mouth when a passenger gave you the wrong change, to the starchy and overbuttered bread rolls from the corner café which filled your stomach, and the ache in your back at six p.m. I knew how it was not to be able to afford groceries, and even medicine, how it was to run out of Tegretol and suffer from fits and wake up in a strange bed in town.

It was a sliding condition, neither here nor there, one I had chosen to leave behind when I got out of Parker's company. So it would be ironic if my son chose to go back there on the basis of the stories I told regarding taxi world. I feared that the same irony was also a judgement from above. Only God's punishments were as symmetrical as the cadences of a taxi poem.

Clubland was where Zeb spent his endless hours and carried around his nineteen-year-old soul in his backpack. The maze extended from Parliament side to the old Turkish bath house at the top of Long Street. Clubland was a portmanteau term, incorporating late-night lounges and teenagers' discos, Red Bull counters, third-floor dancing bars in converted buildings on and around Long, the twenty-four-hour shop at the crowded Engen garage on the corner of Upper Mill where you bought orange juice to chase a tab of x, the Moroccan cafés in town where lines of hookahs stood inside the door, and stoner hang-outs with dusky purple carpets and purple neon signs above their counters.

Clubland was the empire of young and rich-enough Cape-tonians, and of the beautiful, and the ugly, and the light at heart, and, above all, those who had been hardened in the head. It also happened to be Zeb's kingdom. My son knew everyone and their business—who had the pills today and the level of their strength and pharmacological purity, who owned what, who ran away from home, who was saving up for an abortion, who was the up-and-coming DJ, who had the best shipment of records from São Paulo, and, in general, who was carrying what, buying what, burying what. And everybody in Clubland knew Zeb.

Zeb was a watcher. It puzzled me, that my son had found his nineteen-year-old's niche in Clubland. I couldn't see what it was in the great ocean of nineteen- and twenty-year-old's cares and troubles that held his attention. It was so bland and unbelievable.

Clubland had its own revolutionary doctrine. It was about love, music, rebellion, formlessness, playfulness, gender transcendence, hooking up … I just didn't happen to believe a word of it. I had lent enough money to Zeb's friends when they were breaking up with their parents at fifteen and renting rooms in the boarding houses and going into business for themselves. I was immune to giving them sympathy when they moved back home, and moved out again, and borrowed more money from Zeb.

Zeb's interest in Clubland's flotsam-and-jetsam people, with their flotsam-and-jetsam hearts, was genuine enough. He cried with them and rejoiced with them and hustled with them, and, above all, took them seriously. It did make me wonder if Zebulon had the requisite splinter of ice in his heart—the splinter of smoking dry ice which, with its smoky incense unwrapping into the air, created some distance between you and the ceaseless electronic music of all these young persons' sorrows.

In my view, that splinter in the heart was the one thing you needed to be a taxi poet.

When I got home Geromian called because he wanted to celebrate. He couldn't sleep because his tablets were in the suitcase which hadn't arrived. But I didn't want to celebrate my Tuesday victories, or Geromian's existence. I wanted to sleep.

"I'll give you the number for the doctor Helena recommends. I don't go near doctors myself. You can call him the first thing in the morning and he can initial your prescription. If you want, I'll call him for you."

"You're meant to take care of me. Without understanding how it happened, because I am a child at heart, I have become old enough to be dependent on the help of others. If I was in Rio I would call one of my women, sometimes one of my men, and they come to bed with me. It works like a charm to put me out."

I said, "Forget about it. There are limits to what I will do for professional reasons. I've never had the kind of interesting personal life that you enjoyed. And I don't want to start now. And I don't have those feelings."

I had no patience, with Geromian, or with the world. I sounded sterner than I felt. On the other hand, he didn't seem to mind. In his condition of fame there was nothing I could say or do that would sting him. He could be gracious. I could have sworn that his grace was the most refined form of contempt. Nevertheless it made it more difficult to be surly with him, as he deserved.

"Adam, I'm not asking you to do anything. I don't even see you in that light, my dearest. I see you as an equal. I can tell how much Solly valued your individualism, and therefore your refusal to be anybody's man. But I am old enough to want each passing day to go well. And I would like the chance to get some joy, and conversation, out of this one. So let's meet. In Greenpoint, perhaps? It's changed so much, the scent of money everywhere, which is like nail polish. If you come, I can give you the inside stories of the early days of taxi poetry, from the famous rivalries and plagiarisms to the politics of the underground which was inseparable from the literature."

"I heard it from Solly already. And you seem to believe that everybody is copying from you, even Charlotte Monaghan."

"You heard Solly's perspective. Mine is equally deserving of your attention. But well and good. I'll contact Helena Bechman. She gave me her number as a last resort if you let me down."

I walked to the bar. The buildings in town formed a chessboard. Most of the squares were black. There were homeless men under blankets between the walls and the pavement, arguing equally with one another and with the occasional pedestrian. I went past the modelling agencies and the international hotels and embassies, past the planetarium, and then the galleries and furniture showrooms with long windows to show their wares. Further on were the hotels and the restaurant district. You could hear foreign accents at all the outside tables. The Petrobras building in the centre of town, with its neon-green piping, looked more like a magic wand than the headquarters of an international petroleum company.

I doubted all of it. This holiday society remembered nothing, kept no memory of the glories of transportation literature, which made the city of Cape Town itself nearly glorious. The holiday-makers read the eyes of the dice in the casino, disturbed the penguins protecting their eggs on Boulders Beach, listened for the noonday gun, attended to the inscription on the Dias Cross far out on Cape Point in the pouring rain when one felt that the entire peninsula was a ship in a storm. Just as Venice was transformed into a façade, as the punishment for her beauty, so the same thing was happening here.

And the different city, the real city which had been Solly Green-fields' bailiwick, from the curtain shops and Muslim butcheries in Woodstock to Molteno reservoir and the primary-coloured changing huts on Muizenberg beach, was infiltrated by this holiday mood, this product of beauty and superficial existence antithetical to taxi poetry. Soon, everything substantial would be light enough to dissolve in sea spray.

Geromian sat on the balcony at the bar. From there you could see all around from the slopes to the ocean. He wore a red silk shirt and a handkerchief decorated with strawberries in his black blazer. He was talking gallantly to the girl behind the counter. His hands were shaking as he retrieved his drink. In the bar light the amber liquid was radiant.

"Praise be to the gods, Adam, I found a couple of tablets in my pocket which didn't go with the other suitcase. I took a mild sedative, one capsule of Lexomil, but it hasn't kicked in yet. That's why my hands are like this. Pudding, it's beautiful to see you. It's been a long time. This afternoon in my hotel, being here for the first time in years, felt like a lifetime."

"You can get through a lifetime in eight hours," I said.

"Come closer."

When Geromian put his arms around me I could tell that he had also found his cologne. The petrol smell cut right through to my headache. It hadn't been a good day for my body, and the day before hadn't been so good for my soul.

We sat down beside the bar. From here you looked onto the restaurant. There were candles in jars on the tables. A waiter in a white blazer replaced a wine bottle in an ice bucket beside one of the tables. Good-looking women in short skirts, and men in suits, were absorbed in each other and in themselves. At the corner of the next building, almost hidden behind a hedge, was the opalescent surface of the swimming pool. I could hear the water sloshing about inside it.

It wasn't the kind of place you expected to see a taxi poet. It could have been anywhere in the world, in São Paulo, or Milan.

And if you were as famous as Geromian, perhaps you never had to be anywhere in particular. He didn't want to meet his friends and supporters, or return to the places which had been made memorable in his writing. He was more enthusiastic about coming to the bar. It was as if he couldn't imagine a return journey.

I hadn't been looking forward to the conversation. But for some reason, after finishing his drink, and maybe because of the sedative, Geromian was polite.

"Your son, Zebulon, how is he?"

"Zeb's good. Well, he's not bad, considering his age. He's nineteen, nineteen and three-quarters, which is almost the same age I was when I had him. I always do that calculation—where is he, compared to wherever was I at the same age. I can finally understand my feelings, at whatever point, by seeing the same feelings and emotions develop in him. He's far beyond me. He even has the good sense not to fall in love with his best friend Antonia, who you will meet on Thursday if everything goes according to plan. I was never so wise."

"Is that a fact?"

I didn't believe, in principle, that a man like Geromian considered my existence or that of any other individual or really believed that life continued in his absence. But I could also see that the principle was wrong, at an intellectual level, because a taxi poet kept sympathy with all the different forms of life to practise his profession properly. Taxi poetry connected to all the world, to the pebble underfoot and the silver tree on Table Mountain and the old woman hunched over her grocery bag from Shoprite, by rays of sympathy and interest.

Even if the sympathy in Geromian had deteriorated it had left something like curiosity as the residue. I was even more surprised that I would confide in him. I didn't need to be grateful. It had been that kind of a day, thanks to Geromian, and he had imposed himself on me. Moreover, I hadn't been able to talk, not in a real way, since Solly's funeral. I had lost my proper words since Solly's death. So I went on.

"I really didn't understand human nature before Zeb arrived. I didn't have much sympathy with people as such. Now I have a much better understanding, more sympathy, since I can see the layers that one individual is made out of."

"They tell me what you say is true. I never had children myself because I could not justify adding another person to the planet. I don't regret it. It would have been one way to express myself while I have a thousand. And what is our friend Zebulon going to do with his life?"

"Believe it or not, Zeb's still in his first year at the Jose da Silva Perreira Institute. He's got it in his head that he wants to be a sliding-door man, as I told you this morning."

"Not the best idea. If I had to do it again, today, with the transport sector as it's evolved, I would choose differently. I would go into entertainment. It's not the same as when we started, when there was a kind of innocence, and even a kind of glamour, and political idealism. Today it's about money, and power, and which sliding-door man is going to become a taxi Jesus."

"I just can't seem to talk him out of it. I realise I've never persuaded anybody in my life, especially not Zeb out of everybody."

For a minute I thought Geromian was about to cry. I didn't know why the news about Zebulon would move him to tears. Maybe it was his missing suitcase. Then he became interested in another topic.

"I knew Solly Greenfields pretty well in the old days, better than most people would know. In those days, it would have taken more than six bullets. Who knows, in his whole life, how many bullets were fired in his direction? Tell me something now, what was the ceremony like? How did they finally bury Solly?"

"As a Muslim. They did a Muslim ceremony."

"I knew him first as a Jew, you realise. Then, as a Baha'í, when he joined the Baha'í Faith Temple. Finally, when the Special Branch picked me up, I heard from my cell that Solly Greenfields had converted to Hinduism. I suppose it was fitting, in that he was clearly comfortable with the existence of many gods. At that point in time, as far as most of us in the movement were concerned, Trotsky and Lenin were the solution and the final word."

"Is that so?"

"Remember that Marxism-Leninism put us in a unique place in society. They argued from a scientific perspective. They saw the transport sector as the nexus between the economic base and the cultural superstructure. Religion was purely the opiate of the masses. We couldn't start from scratch, theoretically, because we didn't have all the mental firepower. Trotsky and Lenin and Bukharin provided us with a particular way of understanding our situation. We heard about the theory of transport from the authorities in Moscow and Jerusalem and Birmingham and wherever else, including the Brazilian left. So that was what we believed. Whereas, from the start, Solly wanted to find his own path."

"Yes, imagine that."

After that, I closed my ears and opened my eyes. It was a relief. I couldn't bear hearing another syllable. Geromian's stupid speech was the drone of a stupid engine, an engine of egoism no more mindful than the 1200cc Toyota which had brought us into Cape Town that morning.

This other engine had roared into life at the minute of Geromian's birth. It had never been quiet since then, even for a minute, except when the man to which it was attached happened to be asleep. I wished I could pull out its valves. I didn't know why God would put an engine into some of his creations, a soul into others.

Moreover, I thought Gerome was making a riddle out of Solly's death, a joke even, while Solly was shipwrecked in the Parow burial ground. When you came down to it, whether the responsible party was a burglar or a government agent, whether it was five bullets or six bullets, there was no mystery to what had happened.

In the final analysis Solly had died of an underlying condition, which I was now able to spell out for myself. In a city defined by the taxi bosses and the Taxi Owners Association, by Congress Party cadres and their equivalents in the academy, a man like Solly Greenfields was too pure to be allowed to live.

That was Solly's underlying condition, purity, his purity of soul and heart and language. He hadn't been able to compromise, with his verses, his views on adverbs, or the Road Safety Council. It was this purity that had doomed him, just as diabetes would undo Parker, and my tendency to throw in a final word would, at some point in the future, prove to be my own comeuppance. There was something special about Solly, not always likeable, not entirely agreeable to an ordinary spirit, which meant that the establishment wanted to crush him out of existence. It was the same hot, unreliable, sweet-and-sour property which came out in every line he composed.

That my companion couldn't imagine this fact to be true, and cared more about his father and the imaginary and long-ago culture of Clarens, made my chest tight. I wanted to fall dead on the table in front of him. The hysteria rose from my heart, like mercury shooting up in a thermometer. I would have liked to howl in Geromian's face. At the same time, in some other part of my heart, I was calmer than before.

The reason I kept silent, though, had less to do with Geromian or the global standing of Portuguese and Brazilian culture. The truth was, I was too judgemental about people. Geromian didn't mean to subject me to his obnoxious living strength, or even, as this evening had proved, entangle me in his weakness and hopelessness. I should forgive his weakness as I wished to forget about his strength. Geromian, Parker, Zeb's mother Mona, even Solly Greenfields, even Antonia the student from Mocímboa da Praia who was more beautiful in spirit than in the flesh, were manifesting themselves. They had their way of doing things. They had their path. They weren't doing whatever they did to get in my face.

If anything, the situation was the reverse. The aggression came from me. They were innocent. I was the one who wanted to pull out their valves, to stomp on their stupid engines and sing, to stick my angry hands in their ears.

I couldn't say where this desire came from, maybe from the other side of the moon where new wishes and desires are devised. Nor could I predict where it would lead. But it was sure to go somewhere soon.

Something new, and dangerous, I decided, had started at Solly Greenfields' funeral—this dark clock which had begun to chime, this dark and spellbinding music, this dark fluid which flowed out of me in every minute of each hour.

WEDNESDAY

~

I COULDN'T reach Zeb who was trying to reach me. The receiver rang through the middle of my dream, which had to do with Marmalade, and a spoonful of strawberry jam. It took a minute to get to the telephone from across the bed. By then Zeb had left a message to call him.

When I dialled back I got the static on the answering machine. I imagined my son listening to my voice and placing his hands in his pockets because, on second thoughts, he didn't want to explain anything to his father.

That was Zeb Ravens, in his most recent incarnation. I'd encountered it with increasing frequency in recent months, until it had all but replaced the host personality. It got into a predicament and called me because, if you knew something about getting into difficulties, you might also have learned how to get out of them. Once it had my attention, however, it turned around and pretended I didn't exist.

Yet I longed for Zeb's messages even if, as usual, they just concerned one of his friends. Aside from Antonia, Zeb only had friends in need. Someone who took one too many capsules was a friend of Zeb the minute the last pill went down. Someone who was caught for shoplifting in a Cavendish boutique was a friend, as was someone who needed to pay for a girlfriend's abortion. Zeb made friends at a prodigious rate. Far as I knew, there wasn't a person who didn't adore him, apart from his father.

I found myself driving Zeb's new best friend to the Netcare clinic to have a drip put up, or writing a cheque, or persuading a constable to lose a docket. I had some idea, from working for Parker's company, how to deal with enemies. I even thought that, when you were as serious about reversing entropy as any good transport poet, there was the necessity to create enemies. But I couldn't manage having so many new friends.

If there was one thing Zeb was serious about, it was his friends. I listened to him recite their misfortunes with such gravity, treating a shoplifting charge or an unwanted pregnancy as if it was the end of the world and nobody had been caught in a similar situation before, as if the meaning of decolonisation was simply that, on the ironwork balcony of a bar on Long Street, a new friend was free to put the wrong tablet in his mouth. When Zeb deigned to tell me about these incidents I felt that he was describing the plot of some disaster movie. There was a thrill in his voice as if the *Poseidon* were going down.

If it happened to be his father sinking with the ship, however, Zeb would avert his eyes from the embarrassment. He hadn't said a word to me about Solly's murder although he knew we had been close. I was disappointed in his telepathy. It was the kind of situation where if you continued to think about it, you would just break your head.

I tried to keep Zeb's difficulties, his borrowed difficulties, in perspective, something I always had to borrow. I just didn't have to borrow more problems. They arrived entangled, the one with the other and, more often than not, in threes and fours. You couldn't solve one without taking care of four, and you couldn't solve four without fixing two, and so on. I had never been good at undoing knots and preferred it when I could tie different things together so that they could never come undone.

This morning I worried about Marmalade as well. The poor animal was moribund, shabbier and bushier and madder than the day before. The only sign of life on this Wednesday morning was his thick orange-and-white sideburns rising and falling, ever so gently, as he sat in front of the hot-water heater ... small lion, small Buddha. He could sit there for hours, content despite his pains, while the heater ticked as if it was purring back.

While waiting for the geyser to heat up I watched Marmalade and tried to decide what to do about him. There were no good options. I put my things into my backpack and noticed Zeb's packet again. That was what he must have called about.

When I got out of the shower and dried myself, Marmalade had not moved from the heater. Nothing interested him. He didn't investigate his bowl when I refilled it, didn't take an interest in the mynah birds, which stood impudently in the window box and shrieked out of their conical bodies.

When there was time, I would put butter on his paws, place him in the cat cage and take him to the vet. If Marmalade was stingy about his nine lives, he was lucky I was so busy. At the vet he would have received an injection of pentobarbital to stop his small lion's heart and never have the breath to complain about the prick in his side.

I wished my old friend was here to advise. Solly had been full of wisdom about his cats. It was he who applied butter to a cat's paws when he wanted to lure it into the cage to take along on some excursion. While the animal cleaned its paws you could push it through the gate. Other people used a dab of cream, or the yellow, seed-flecked gooseberry jam from the corner café. Using butter was a small tradition of Solly's, one of many which were recalled in his taxi poetry. It was a small tradition also that cats were the familiars of a taxi poet. Supposedly, unlike Zeb and me, they knew each other's thoughts. It might have been so, but Solly still relied on a pat of butter, not telepathy. And I had never thought to share my mind with another animal.

Marmalade wasn't about to feed himself. I inserted a pellet of cat food into his mouth, and then another, and another. He didn't move but accepted the biscuits onto his humid tongue. Up close he whistled rather than breathed.

"How are you doing, Marmalade? Cat got your tongue?"

Marmalade's owner was fond of bad puns, but the inclination hadn't descended to the animal. He didn't look up. I could hardly find his body with my hands. The warm and still living worm of him had almost disappeared inside the frightful orange bush. I noticed, for the first time, that Marmalade produced the odour of shrimp shells.

"You're not clean, you know that? I don't know what I should do about you. I should give you a bath. I could put you in the washing machine and turn you into a rug."

Solly would have laundered his cat, despite Marmalade's palpable fear of bath water, which grew when the slightest drop landed on him. Then Solly would trim his hair with nail scissors, and sweeten his breath, and clean the half orange-and-white stub of an ear he had left from a brawl with a tomcat, and brush through his orange hair with the heavy tortoiseshell brush which he could never use on his own bald brown head.

I had some feeling for Marmalade rising in my heart, because he had once, and not so very long ago, been a sleek and beautiful cat, lazy, and lovely. He fought with other cats and hunted butterflies from the wall covered with broken bottle tops around the back of the house.

Marmalade was the lamp Solly rubbed when he wanted a taxi poem to come out. He composed in the bath with his arm out the side so that he could keep hold of Marmalade, or whichever cat it happened to be.

There were drawbacks to being in too close proximity to a taxi poet. Eventually, after a decade or so, Solly's rubbing seemed to rub each animal out. He would be replaced, silently and with no acknowledgement from his owner regarding his passing, by a much younger cat which could have been picked off the street on a whim or taken down from a balcony pipe or stolen from one of the backyards which lay along his route back from the bus shelter. If you were familiar with the cycles of Solly's work you saw a period of sudden new inventions and new associations and speculations with the arrival of a new animal in his house. For the mathematically minded, the great Solly Greenfields went through about two animals for every three collections.

I silently promised his old cat that I would bring him a tin of sardines on that very afternoon, when and if I came back from Parker's, and place each gleaming, needle-tongued brown fillet on his tongue.

It would have to be a red tin of Lucky Star sardines, or pilchards in tomato sauce picked up from the Somali shop. Marmalade had no partiality for snoek, wouldn't even steal it from the table because of the bones. Solly never managed to convince him, or any cat, of the superior virtues of the snoek.

Everything nonetheless converted into everything else, and so the almost boneless pilchards became the dismal orange hair on Marmalade's back which, in turn, became an electrical tingling in Solly's hand finally converted into a taxi poem on the side of one

Hi-Ace. In the transport sector nothing went in a straight line, especially not the taxi poets.

It was in the hope of finding Zeb that I went up to the Perreira Institute, as well as pretending to teach my course on some aspects of transport versification. Zeb, I knew, had a seminar with Gil Etteh around the same time. The switchboard tried to put through a call from Geromian, which I ducked.

Preparations were underway for Thursday's ceremony. On my way to put my head into Gil's seminar and haul out my son, my Telemachus, I passed the main auditorium, where a technician was standing on a ladder and checking the blue lights along the front of the chamber.

Zeb wasn't in class. Nor was Gil. I asked but nobody had seen either of them. Gil was late almost as a matter of religious observance, but it wasn't like Zeb to be absent. Plus I had a class of my own in fifteen minutes.

Helena stopped me as I came out of the door. The students had to make their way around us to get out, minnows around sharks. They had backpacks, like Zeb, and I began to wonder why he hadn't simply carried his parcel home in it. It was unlike him to trust me with anything, big or small.

Helena wasn't pleased to see me. There was something particular about her biochemistry which could have developed at the University of Lisbon where they cultivated colonies of scholars like bacteria. As I diagnosed her, Helena was too serious to take pleasure from the minutiae of life. Only the grandest aspects of life, nothing resembling the tiny bones of a snoek, gave her a short sticky ripple of happiness.

"Did you do something with your hair?"

"Adam, now is really not the time for flattery. And, with me, it's quite likely that the time will never come. Sebastian has never even given me flowers. On to the practical issues, if you don't mind. You ignored the switchboard just now. They forwarded Geromian to me. His prescriptions have to be filled. I arranged for the name of a doctor who can sign them. You can't take chances like that. In future, and the future is limited to the next three days, if you make sure that whatever Gerome wants he gets, and take his calls, I will be most appreciative. And, before you begin to speak, you don't have to make an excuse."

"I wasn't about to make an excuse, Helena. I was on my way to find someone urgently."

I wasn't the one who needed an excuse. Geromian needed an excuse to be alive. I was almost angry with Helena too. She had placed me in five days of bondage. Someone like Solly would never have accepted it. He didn't like to be in bondage. It was part of why you didn't find a taxi poet working for an institution or corporation, except for a taxi company where they didn't mind rough-hewed people. Geromian never suffered that way, even if he talked at length about bondage in his memoirs. Maybe people either liked to be tied up or to be the one doing the tying, and it was because of this that existence was full of knots.

Neither of them, Solly nor Geromian, had Helena to reckon with. She was the most efficient agent Nemesis ever deployed. Not three minutes had elapsed since I ignored Geromian's call and she was there to upbraid me. Oedipus would hardly have been king for a day. There wasn't a mistake, no matter how minor, during my term of employment at the Institute that I got away with. If I misspelled my name on a form which went across her desk, or if I didn't fill in the date, or if the month and the day were reversed, it would come back to me with the slash of a red pen. With Helena, one kind of bondage was much like the other one.

PROBLEM #4: Just because I had always done, and for no other reason, I felt the familiar desire to cry in Helena's presence. But we were both professionals. We could keep up the pretence that I wasn't brushing a tear out of my eye.

She continued. "Meanwhile, on a more pleasant subject for you, I am under an obligation to you for the change in thinking you imposed on the third-semester students."

"Antonia turned out to be more rational than you credit."

"Young women make the worst revolutionaries, don't they? They pretend to be such purists but without the backbone. In any event, it is sorted. They have unofficially postponed their boycott. Also, we have agreed to an amnesty on library fines, which I am happy to grant because none of them know the way to the library. Let every book never be returned. I wanted to show you my gratitude."

"Say nothing more."

I wasn't sure how much more gratitude Helena could show. I had perhaps breached the extent of it by continuing on the faculty despite her advice to the contrary. Unlike Parker, she was uncomfortable with incurring an obligation, even if it cost me nothing to reason with Antonia. Indeed, it was a pleasure to have the excuse to be around Antonia.

And there was a kind of pleasure, too, in Helena's company. In her discomfort, which she tried to banish, she was more lovely than ever. She was middle-aged and lovely and even lonely. Her eyes were darker and greener than I had registered. But they weren't sharp enough to devise a plan to encompass all the possibilities of existence. No intern who had to catch the drift of a taxi poem would have made the same mistake about life and straight lines.

I doubted her husband saw to the lonely core of her being, which was a command economy. Sebastian was even more successful than Helena, prodigally successful in institutional terms. He was generally liked around the university for his sunny and open demeanour, and universally distrusted for the same reason. So he wouldn't know how to untie a knot in Helena because he didn't have knots of his own.

"All right. I've communicated my thanks. Now I have to move. There are a lot of loose ends to tie up prior to Geromian's lecture. By the way, your contract is up soon. Next week, or just before, we will negotiate. Let's cast our minds towards this coming Friday as a possible date. There are some points we need to settle. In the meantime make sure that Geromian's life goes well."

"I look forward to talking, Helena. By Friday I hope to be free of all my worries."

I was late for my class. I put my backpack on the table and quoted some examples of Charlotte Monaghan's taxi villanelles on the blackboard. It wasn't like it had been between Solly and me in his kitchen, although the clock on the wall of the classroom had stopped like the timer on Solly's oven.

I told them to look over Geromian's work in anticipation of Thursday night and that the taxi companies would be rougher places than the Institute and to remember the example of Solly Greenfields and a number of additional facts I must have told them before. I read out loud from Solly's old ballad that remembered the unhappy history of the transport system:

We came here then, to work upon the roads.
We were brought to this place, Victoria West.
There we were lifting stones, up to our chests,
were rolling them away. We had to carry earth,
loaded in a hand-barrow, and throw it out again.
We had to do this many days, we and the Koranas.
We had to throw it in a wagon, push the wagon wheels.

There for many days we loaded earth, unloaded earth,
we and the Koranas. And when they took us back
to jail each night, sheep's flesh is what we ate.

As I was reading, I put my hand into my backpack and found
Zeb's package. It had entirely escaped my mind. I needed to give it
back to him, if I could find him. The students were allowing me to
talk to myself. Someone at the back, who could have been a joker,
put up his hand. He had two small earrings in one ear and a dyed
white slash in his hair which reminded me of a fox's pelt.

"I'm sorry. What's the question again?"

"This is the third semester, my friend. You're meant to provide
your own questions. I can't give you the questions. This is an
institute, not a nursery school."

"You already told us, in the first class, that you didn't have any
answers either."

I said, "I don't remember saying that. It's not impossible that
I did. But it doesn't mean I was right about it. Well, I give up.
Make sure to get to Geromian's early work before the lecture on
Thursday so that it has some meaning for you. I wouldn't bother
so much after, say, 1979."

It was hopeless to be in a classroom, for me and also for the
third-semester students. They should have been sent to Woodstock
to touch Solly Greenfields, while he was around, and to brush his
hair in the bath and to rub the same animal as Solly did and thus
receive some jolt of his electricity.

If the students had no electricity of their own, of course, I was
to blame. And so was Helena Bechman, for believing that an
institute for taxi poetry should be run like a railroad.

Today, I saw the problem without being able to fix it. I couldn't
think how to get the current flowing between us. Either the new
generation could create sparks of their own, or they couldn't, and

they couldn't see these sparks in their dreams or feel the presence of them in the air.

And maybe I wouldn't hear if there was a crackle. Maybe my ears were too full of new white hairs, which had emigrated from Solly Greenfields.

On my way out of the seminar I ran into Antonia. I always had ears for her.

She was going into the same classroom and didn't look as tired as before.

At the same time, I saw, she wasn't happy to see me. She must have felt as if I had exploited her to get around the boycott on Helena's behalf. If I had indeed used her to postpone the revolution it was only because the finest persons were the most usable. It was a mark of affection that I went to her. She was as useful as she was beautiful. I wanted to tell her as much.

"I'm so grateful, my dearest Antonia, about the boycott. I don't believe I have ever seen Helena Bechman pleased with me until today. I want to say one thing, on a matter of principle. I didn't intend to strong-arm you into calling it off. It was only that I trusted you as the right person to appeal to. In future, if you and the third-semester students want to call a boycott, I promise to stay away in solidarity."

"No problem."

"Don't you volunteer at the Road Safety Council? It isn't safe to be idealistic, as Solly said."

"I was taught to take care of myself. Nobody's going to take advantage."

"But be careful. Someone out there has a gun and is prepared to use it. By the way, I can't find Zeb today again. But I don't want to make you responsible for the existence of my son. So I am not even going to ask where he is. If you happen to see him, tell him to call home. You may be the one person he listens to."

Oh, Antonia, Antonia Chirindza! I wanted to be in solidarity with you. I wasn't even in love with your beauty and accent, your stern revolutionary virtue, and your way of handling me as if I was a counter-revolutionary. I simply wanted to be as close to you as Zebulon. Through you the current would pass from Zeb to me and back.

Instead, oh, Antonia, you gave me a strange look and hurried into a classroom where, even in the worn old grey Terylene carpet, there wasn't one amp of static electricity.

I was already late for Parker. Parker valued punctuality, which he defined as saving other people's seconds just as you saved your own change. I was up the mountain but had to go to town side to arrive at the main taxi rank on Grand Parade adjacent to the municipal buildings and the converted drill hall. It was a stone's throw from Parliament. Demonstrators on Grand Parade occasionally tried to prove it.

On Grand Parade it was business as usual. Business as usual, in this part of the world, was chaos. The same Hi-Aces were queuing at the exit. Others were parked, pounding their big muddy speakers through open doors, Brenda Fassie pop against the same old kwaito against hip-hop and gospel and Sufi devotional music and the presenter on Cape Talk who disappeared and reappeared from different sliding doors as I went along. The money here might be made in transportation but that didn't mean the Taxi Owners Association invested in the facilities.

People were shoving past me to get to their connections, hurrying in every direction, talking loudly from the window of one taxi to another, and eating and drinking and shouting and looking for change or their telephones in the bottom of their pockets and handbags.

A counter served those far-too-floury factory-made steak-and-kidney pies which people consumed with tomato sauce and vinegar while standing. At desks and tables between the rows of Toyotas one could obtain the services of a palm reader, telephonist, cobbler, translator, conveyancer, bride-price negotiator, adult circumciser, or the typist who balanced his machine on his lap and, from a purple inkpad, stamped your identity book in the name of Home Affairs, barbers who used electric shavers and spread newspapers underneath their chairs, and a person who would set a charm to scare an immigrant out of a shop or another property you coveted.

You could get to Robertson on Rosenstein's taxis, to the rural areas on Molefe's, to Bellville and Simon's Town naval base with Mrs Rooknodien, and to anywhere on the Cape Flats, from Gatesville Shopping Centre to Wembley Road House, with Parker who, as he liked saying, had his own game of Monopoly separate from Parker Brothers.

I wasn't familiar anymore with the taxis Parliament side. I stood in the road and asked the drivers where to find a Parker's taxi. A Hi-Ace which had been reversing slowly came back much faster. It ran over my shoe and it would have run over me if I hadn't stepped back. I thought it had broken the bones in my foot. My boot was as flat as a pancake.

I would have run after it as far as the red light and scolded the sliding-door man but he had a Gorgon's face which didn't react to the incident and would simply have turned me into stone, if he hadn't pulled out a truncheon from beneath the seat and broken the bones in my hand also.

In the same moment, however, I saw that it was one of Parker's Toyotas. I allowed one of the passengers to stretch out an arm and found myself pulled up. It was a Hi-Ace Super-T, which held up to twenty-eight passengers with no fear of the afterlife.

The kombi had a reinforced side step. You could stand on it if you kept your other arm inside the door. The blocks around Parliament began to roll by and I could see the waiter at the wine bar pouring a bottle into three flutes at an empty table on the pavement. A Golden Arrow bus thundered slowly as a mastodon across the intersection. There were no passengers on board.

I was prepared to stay out there, with my injured foot, until Belthorn Estate came around again. Instead I was summoned inside. It was the Gorgon of a sliding-door man who had stone in his voice as well as in his expression. He spoke friendly words but there was no friendliness in them.

"Come a little front, my brother. There's space to spare over here. Make yourself comfortable. Do us all a favour. Sit more front. There are only four people on that second bench. Get that woman to move over. As for you, madam, it wouldn't do you any harm to go on a diet and drink skim milk if you want to ride on the taxi. Drink skim milk and save the extra calories. You never know when they will come in handy."

Inside the Hi-Ace we belonged to taxi world, which was different in its basic logic to the world of houses and suburbs and universities and private companies. I had left it behind me but it was immediately familiar—the passengers with their parcels and grievances and the small change of their conversation which they passed back and forth as if they were feeling for the timbre of each coin, the tape player turned to the loudest setting and the graphic equaliser with ten buttons slung underneath the dashboard, the spirituous Dettol scent in the checked upholstery, even the gold lamé shirt tight on the arms of the sliding-door man who was organising the tickets.

I pushed the large woman aside. She moved the shopping bag

under the bench to her side. The coins came back, handed from passenger to passenger, and then to the woman who didn't take skim milk and was still boiling with anger as if a saucepan of the full-fat version was running over, until the money was returned to my hands. I didn't care to count it. I had a good reason not to do so. If you counted your coins, I believed, you also counted your words, and therefore, you were unsuited for the taxi-poet profession. It was one good reason that a sliding man like this one, in his gold shirt, would never graduate to the next stage. Yet Solly had counted his coins.

"I haven't seen you on Parker's taxi, my brother, which is, no question, the finest and most reliable taxi service available. But you can see for yourself. Oh, my brother, where are you headed?"

"Belthorn side," I said, "where the old bioscope used to be, the one they showed Bruce Lee movies at. I don't know if you remember that one. They used to show double features every public holiday. I think before that it was a drive-in."

We were underway. My sliding friend smiled. He wasn't a Gorgon any longer. I saw that the driver wore the same short-sleeve gold shirt as he did. It gave their dark necks and hands a metallic sheen, as if they had been spray-painted. The sliding man and his colleague must have bought them on a two-for-one special, maybe at the Greenfields factory outlet in Salt River, which was started by Solly's brother.

Town rolled past, the Woolworths building, and then the train station and the square outside it. From the motorway bridge I saw the cable car running on its trapeze wire high above the heads of the many horses pacing along the slopes of the mountain.

We were on Kromboom Road, passing the neighbourhood super-markets, the Anglican schools, and churches, and then butcheries, hardware stores, and distributors for car parts. Because of the way the routes were divided through the municipality, Parker's taxis went back along Kromboom and past his house before they went on to destinations on the far side of Athlone Stadium.

Nobody was talking except the sliding-door man and the driver. They had different, but equally vehement, opinions about soccer and the Seven Stars Football Club. The driver was losing the fight, having his views pushed back slowly but surely. It was impossible to contend with the argumentative skills of a sliding-door man, who pushed your words back across the table as if it was a carrom board.

That was the other reason a sliding-door operator only rarely became a taxi poet. He spoke an ordinary word and it sounded like a curse. He moved the words around in his mouth as if he were chewing a Wilson's Toffee. I could predict this sliding man's opinions about women and Shangaans, whether he preferred Galeto's Portuguese chicken to Nando's, whether he would be at Galaxy on a Thursday evening and which floor he frequented, because I had been there on the same Thursdays.

Like the taxi companies, the sliding-door men had their own game of Monopoly. They had a monopoly on sitting around at the front of the Hi-Ace and observing other people's faults. They had a monopoly on having all the stupid answers to every stupid question. And, you know, I counted myself as the worst offender of the lot.

I said, "Will you answer a question for me?"

"My brother, there is no harm in questions, isn't it? You've come to the right taxi. They tell me I have an answer for everything."

"In that case you are unlike any sliding-door man I've come across. So tell me, young as you are, have you ever heard the name of Solly Greenfields?"

"Solly the moffie? He wasn't a fan of the female species. Didn't he begin the Road Safety Council with their idea of putting points on your licence and saying this one can drive and this one cannot?

In a free country, who will accept that? No, he is not popular over here, true's God. He was a taxi poet for Parker at one stage. Did I say something wrong?"

"You could say that, yes."

My hands trembled. I was flaring into anger again, as if he had blown on the coals which had been smouldering against Zeb and Helena. I could have been a Gorgon but I couldn't meet his eyes.

It was my son, however, who caused the most aggravation, not this man on the seat in front of me. What kind of sliding adventure did Zeb need to make of his life? There was nothing to romanticise. It wasn't even Clubland, although they wore the same shirts. Zeb was too delicate, too mysterious in his soul, to rub shoulders with a man in a cheap gold shirt and eat his front-seat lunch of an ordinary factory pie.

At this moment, with all the pain in my foot which had as many small bones in it as a snoek, I missed being a driver. I missed something about my life which had never come to pass, and perhaps what I missed was the same innocence which I demanded from the souls of other individuals and didn't have myself. But I wanted Zeb to possess it, in defiance of the degradations of Clubland.

The weather wasn't good anymore. The taxi turned into the district of warehouses, and clinics, and petrol garages, and electricity substations. At the stadium there was a match, and a new burst of rain fell through the tangerine floodlights on the players. Between the public buildings were long lines of brown brick suburban houses protected by heavy iron gates and grey cement walls. These railway workers and boilermakers and municipal bookkeepers and teachers and assistants at the millionaires' churches newly arrived on every second corner, and beggars who were twice as frequent, were the secret heroes of Solly's taxi poetry.

I had another secret which I would never convey to my sliding friend who wasn't a friend. On the side of the Hi-Ace, these railway workers and boilermakers and schoolchildren from the Catholic and Muslim academies were reading, through the sliding rain, a taxi sonnet which happened to be written by the author of Zeb's existence.

I couldn't rub a taxi poem out of Marmalade's back. I wasn't a natural. The images came with terrible slowness and a line would never come right until it had been hammered and melted into shape. For me, a taxi poem could occupy weeks and even months, cutting and turning on the lathe, many hours and even days of a dead heart which wouldn't give out a spark of electricity.

This one taxi poem came at a single blow. It had taken me an hour and I couldn't believe my eyes, or my ears. I tuned and retuned it, yet I couldn't improve on a single vibration. It had been born perfect, like a butterfly, the only butterfly I ever created so suddenly. Its wings beat inside my hands and demanded to escape, I felt like a magician. Solly had been clear, during my apprentice year, that it was only blind luck, not some current I could rely on to flow through my hands and produce one butterfly after the other.

I was extremely nervous when I showed it to Solly. He looked at it in the tub, his heavy legs spread out to their full extent, and handed the typescript back to me without covering up his private parts. He didn't suggest any corrections when he read through it, which I counted as his closest approach to praise. At the end of his perusal he almost let it fall in the very hot water, which I also counted as the greatest compliment.

It might have been mere clumsiness. Solly was awkward but he could also be entirely unconscious of his physical existence. I remembered his penis floating like a sea creature under the water. It was attended by a tangle of hair, snow white, like the hair on his pillowy belly, and ethereal, like smoke from a fire that long ago burned out.

Later Solly gave it to Parker, who was pleased himself, and not just because Solly told him to be, I think. Parker memorised the words and, in my presence, repeated them to sundry of his friends and connections, as if they were a spell which would prevent him putting on another pound.

It was Parker's magic, more than Solly himself, which let a taxi poem change its form. First it was in the shape of the cigarette paper I put in Solly's hands and which wound up with Parker. The same taxi poem was painted on a 1979 Hi-Ace above a chromium hubcap that looked like a colander. The text of the taxi poem, like the hubcaps, must have been transferred to this minibus when the previous one broke down and was replaced with a loan from the recapitalisation programme.

So it was only a Toyota and only travelled the route from Parliament side to Belthorn Estate, not the most glamorous destination. It was only a taxi sonnet, constructed on a passing resemblance between the Hi-Ace and the breadbox in a Simon's Town spaza shop and the frigate on the dry dock on the same side with its rusting keel exposed.

So it was only nothing. Taxi poetry made nothing happen, a nothing that was nevertheless a happening. Nonetheless, for the first time in many months in the midst of Parker's taxi, I sounded some new lines out loud. They were intended for the snoek poem, long overdue and now never to be deciphered by the intended recipient in his bath as he groped himself and almost dropped the cigarette foil on which it was printed:

The snoek has no teeth tiny enough
By which to grasp its condition
That, in my modest opinion, is rough,
Like the N2 taking me off to perdition,
And stuff.

This snoek poem would incorporate all the topics of existence, from the grand philosophy of the dark universe, ninety-nine percent of which transcended our perception, down to the humble bone which came out in your mouth.

This same snoek poem would explain how I reached into the backpack on my lap and unwrapped Zeb's package during the ride to Parker's and how I found in it something which had the shape of a gun. I thought that my hand had been singed as I touched it.

I reached into the backpack again. I didn't want to take it out. It still had the shape and weight of a gun. I could even feel what felt like a barrel and a trigger. I wouldn't think about it again until I got back from Parker's house. I didn't want to have anything on my mind about Zeb when I talked to Parker because he had an unerring ability to pry out whatever happened to be in your thoughts. He would know I had a gun on my mind.

Next to the power station in Belthorn Estate wasn't the first place I would choose to live. If you knew Parker's operation you could see why he never moved anywhere better, such as a palace in Bantry Bay with the ocean in the windows, or one of the properties in Constantia preferred by members of the Congress Party for reasons of privacy.

Parker was a politician and would never let a quarrel develop if he could help it, having this old-fashioned virtue of keeping his many relationships going, something like sewing with a thimble. He knew the names of each of the sliding-door men he employed, enquired after their wives and mothers and children and cousins, and delivered a Christmas box to every one of their houses.

Depending on your station, this Christmas box would contain something different. I had received a frozen-solid box of Pennington sardines, and on another occasion a box of Yemeni dates which contained the remnants of wasps that you could pick out from the black contents. Once I got five tins of Dulux paint that I later sold to the Muizenberg hardware store.

Parker preferred for the other person to be in his debt, as if he had even given this individual permission to live but would never charge for oxygen. This was a point of difference. I grew up without owing much of anything to anybody. I relied on myself and, later, on Solly's judgement. Solly paid an overdue account for me at Lunat's Pharmacy around the corner and it was the last I heard of it. He had tact.

Parker made a point about obligation even when he wasn't making it a point. I didn't like the sensation. Not having much of a father in the first place, I didn't necessarily want a second father in the shape of Parker. It made me feel I was being strangled.

You were more likely to be electrocuted if you crossed Parker. It was rumoured that Parker's mechanic had once connected the battery in a Hi-Ace to a pair of hissing leads and sent the electricity through the head of a sliding-door man who gave short money. Nobody in the whole of Belthorn Estate heard anything, or reported a relative missing, or saw the fountain of sparks rising above the wall. Nobody came to that house in order to read the electric meter or check the television licence. On occasion, a volunteer from the Road Safety Council pushed a booklet through the mailbox. But that was treated as a prank.

That was the Flats, from the derelict canal to Montague Gardens and Lavender Hill. It contained the great majority of the population of Cape Town who had their own private business. Maybe they had a parent in the hospital, or an account at Checkers collecting interest, or a daughter who wanted to order the material for her matric-dance dress from the tailor shop in Salt River. They didn't have the time to interfere in the business of a taxi company. Not one of them, in my experience, had the ears of a saint, even a fat saint's ability to hear the slightest crackle of suffering at a distance. When it came to a taxi boss, neither did the municipal police listen too closely. They didn't want to strain their ears.

Parker's residence was also his headquarters. The minibuses came to be repaired or parked off on a public holiday, to drop the day's takings, to report the amount of cold-drink money which was distributed to whichever city policeman caught them at the red light on Kromboom Road.

I went around the back of the house, past the workshop where there was a Hi-Ace on blocks. There was a newly installed Dutch door, open at the top. It led into the kitchen of a house where I hadn't been in more years than I wanted to count on two hands. I took off my backpack, made sure it was zipped tight and Zeb's packet was at the bottom, and prepared myself to meet Parker again and all the feelings of my first life.

At the far end of the house, the business of the Taxi Owners Association was underway. I could hear men's voices in the hall although I couldn't make out the words.

I recognised a woman's voice. It was low and roughly tuned, like a viola, and it seemed at first, just when she began to say something, that she was growling.

The viola was a lady of my acquaintance, even if Mrs Rooknodien and I weren't so well acquainted, and she wasn't a lady in the conventional sense. She was Dr Rooknodien's widow. He had been one of the first to run a taxi operation on the grand scale, financing a fleet of two-dozen Microbuses from loans raised against his private clinic.

Maya Rooknodien, as she became, had been in school with me. She was two classes below me. She knew my name and not much else and could hardly have registered when I dropped out. I couldn't have meant much to someone in her league. Whereas I still had the image of her schoolgirl form in my memory banks.

Maya was the subject of intense interest among the male population. Women didn't register with her so much and she didn't necessarily impress other women as gorgeous. It was hard for me to tell sometimes. She had very dark brown hair and a face which was either very beautiful, or else it reminded you of a racoon on account of its sharp bones and eyebrows.

In matric Maya had been lifted out of our sphere altogether by becoming a beauty queen. She quickly married this Dr Rooknodien, who attended such beauty pageants around Athlone in the capacity of judge and sponsor. He was formally engaged as the medical practitioner who vouched for the virginity of the participants.

Then Dr Rooknodien had health problems. He was much older than his bride and, I imagined, had worn himself out judging beauty competitions, which were dangerous to a man's health. He wouldn't have known. His medical qualification had been purchased from a college in British Guiana where he spent three months in a guest house. As a physician, he was about as equipped to heal himself as Solly's country dentist.

Rooknodien passed on three months after his wedding day. He left Maya as one of the very few women to serve on any of the five-hundred-odd regional taxi owners associations. The larger Associations controlled territory containing several million commuters with the gross national product of Botswana. They imported petrol, made spare parts under licence from Toyota and Tata, and ensured the profitability of transport infrastructure. For obvious reasons they were historically a male province. Although there were women who pooled their resources in a stokvel and bought a controlling interest in one Toyota, at her level Maya was unique. Like many others, I believed that she wasn't to be trifled with. After all, Rooknodien had died as a result of too much proximity to her beauty.

I stayed in the small waiting room, taking the opportunity to breathe for the first time since Monday. I was even grateful for Parker's invitation to be there, although I didn't care about the business side of his activities. I didn't have much interest in business at all and didn't see it as the object of a taxi poet's concern. It was why I had never joined the Road Safety Council, despite my admiration for its founder.

I didn't have the same chip on my shoulder as Solly when it came to the management class. They hadn't been born with silver spoons in their mouths. With the exception of Rooknodien, the owners began as fitters and turners, or sliding-door men, or foremen on a building site who borrowed money from Standard Bank or were the beneficiaries of a government programme to aid small business. At most, in the first years under the Congress Party, they might have been the franchise holder for something on the level of a City Pies outlet. They were poor people who simply happened to be rich.

Parker, who was rich, didn't change his taste so he didn't have to replace his wardrobe. Looking around the sitting room I could tell that Parker was as conservative as I remembered, never wanting a chair to be moved from its original position.

So Parker had replaced the lounge suite, but it was the same heavy Morkels furniture, new uncomfortable brown leather couches, and the same piously draped red cloth-covered lamps, like the television cabinet. A jug of lemon water stood on one of the tables, in which the brown seeds had floated to the sides.

On the shelves above the electric fireplace in the big lounge I was sure to discover the same red leather volumes of transport poetry. They would be standing in the same order, with their red tie bookmarks separating the same pages. Parker appreciated taxi poetry, and he loved books, but he didn't necessarily open them.

Parker saw me and came into the lounge. He was wearing a

loose, pale-yellow jersey, yellow pants and beach shoes. He looked healthier, and happier, and even heavier, and more mole-ridden, than at Solly's funeral, and I suppose only the first of those developments should have been a surprise to me. I thought that Parker would live forever, because he already belonged to the undead.

"Glad you accepted my invitation, Ace. I'll organise you a coffee. You have it black with one sugar, if memory serves me correctly. We had to move, but we have finished most of the business. Maya's here, your connection. Who else might you know? Phil Chuboso arrived. Later on, if you can take an extra five minutes out of your Wednesday, I'd like to talk in private."

"It's perfectly fine. I'm at your disposal. I didn't want to interrupt before."

"You wouldn't have interrupted. There were some new routes to distribute, given how quickly the map of the city is changing. And we have to take a position on the legislation which is being considered in Parliament next month. But nothing too dramatic. I leave Sergio to work out the fine detail. I find that I no longer have the patience. Now you'll excuse me. Is anything wrong on your side, Adam?"

"Why should anything be wrong?"

"I thought I saw something in your face. But even as a taxi poet, you understand, for me you have always been difficult to read."

I wasn't sure if it was a compliment. The coffee arrived while I stood in the corner. I wasn't used to being in such exalted company. Even I had ceased to feel Solly's exaltedness because I had counted all the hairs in his ears. The Perreira Institute went around reality in circles. Whereas, in the presence of the Taxi Owners Association, one had the sense of individuals who had established a different relationship to life and death and the very few facts in between which counted. They had power over other people's lives and deaths.

Rosenstein, for instance, was asking Parker a question. He didn't know me but I knew about him. His family was originally from Lithuania. He made unconventional financial arrangements, controlling a number of the Sea Point taxis through a complicated system by which he lent money to buy the minibuses and provided security and insurance without necessarily holding the certificates for each vehicle. He had Somali front men.

Rosenstein had spare eyebrows and a gloomy face, as if he kept a bitter herb in his mouth to remind him of the facts of the world. He had seen far too much to be vain, and maybe too much to be human. Even inside Parker's house, he wore a large hat which would never be doffed. His black suit wasn't clean and looked chalky on the shoulders. I wanted to reach over and dust it off.

As a left-Trotskyite, or Bukharinite, or whatever he was the day you asked, Solly Greenfields was good on the political specifics. He had the scoop on Rosenstein. Despite paying for the eviction of Palestinian families in Jerusalem, when he was in Cape Town, Rosenstein collaborated with the Somalis, involved in their own Hegira.

Together they ran a security company which contracted to the regional taxi owners association and Transnet. Rosenstein organised the equipment, from intercoms to bulletproof vests, while his Somali friends provided the personnel from their community, those sullen men who talked among themselves but never gave away a word to somebody else in any of the eleven languages.

The Somalis had something cultured, past the point of decadence, in their faces. Even when I had ten minutes to spare at a rank which one of them were guarding, I never succeeded in borrowing a word or a sentence. They were supertough and I didn't want to trifle with unnecessary conversation. In common with Rosenstein, and perhaps for reasons that were not so very different, they displayed a certain contempt for their own and other people's lives.

Besides Maya and Rosenstein, there were the legendary last names—Haaze, Molefe, Rodriguez, Chuboso. Molefe and Chuboso were the outsiders, having their base in the rural areas, and having had to force their access to central Cape Town at gunpoint. There had been many casualties among the rival security teams in the resulting conflict. It had taken many months to resolve when I was a driver for Parker, and more than a few paroxysms of violence. Under the terms of a truce imposed by Congress between long-range operators and the municipal companies, the rural companies under Chuboso's direction were now accepted members of the regional taxi owners association.

Rodriguez was another kind of outsider. He arrived in Cape Town following Portugal's Revolução dos Cravos, the Revolution of Carnations, when Lisbon abandoned its possessions on the continent, spawning a dozen insurgencies and sending a hundred thousand Creoles south.

Gabriel Frank Rodriguez had once been the cashier at the Mowbray Mobil. We filled the taxis there, when I was working for Parker, and signed an account book instead of paying in cash. Rodriguez could not have been less interested in culture and refinement. He had just been focused on survival.

When I wasn't looking he bought the Mobil franchise, and then another, and then started managing a fleet of Microbuses out of his Mowbray garage. It happened quickly. Out of nowhere Frank Rodriguez recreated the style of old-money Cape Town. Five years from standing behind the Mobil counter where he sold Fanta and Simba chips, Rodriguez took possession of a winery. He employed the sons of the Malay families, housed in tin barracks on the estate, to operate his taxis.

By some law of increasing good taste, the Fanta led to cheap wine in the box and then good wine in a bottle with a red rose of wax round the collar and then expensive paintings on the walls. Rodriguez had renovated the colonnaded house on the same estate, patronised art critics there, sponsored exhibitions of avant-garde performance and painting, and through his collecting activities took sides in the art-world feud between the Trotskyites and the Bukharinites. No local Congress Party structure could bring about a truce in that rivalry.

While I was drinking coffee in the big lounge Maya came up to me. Her face was flushed, more open, and not as narrow as I remembered when she had been a beauty queen.

For the first time I could imagine Maya as a part of travelling humanity, an aunt, or a friend, or the lady without a name beside you on the taxi who was taunted by the sliding-door man to drink less full-cream milk.

I saw she wasn't wearing a wedding ring. That same moment I saw that her hands were different. They looked as if she had been in the bath too long. Were mine so different also? Yesterday my hands had been as beautiful in their way, a taxi poet's fine and speaking and intelligent hands, as her schoolgirl figure. Except for Zebulon, they were the one thing I was proud of. I put down my cup on the sideboard and steadied myself.

"I see you're friends with Parker again. This is a reconciliation I am glad to witness," she said.

"You think we're truly friends again?"

"I insisted on it. After Solly's funeral I spoke to Parker about it in the bluntest of terms. I stated to him that you used to be extremely close. You were the one taxi poet, apart from Solly, whose career he should support. Now you are our man on the inside of this Institute where I am getting great interns. I wasn't so arrogant as

132

to believe that any speech of mine would have an effect on Parker. But today he announced that you were coming to the house. I'm not saying I'm behind it. I just saw the logic behind it."

It was the same situation with Maya, who was just as she had been in school time. She had the habit of coming to the point too directly, as if she was cutting something between you and her with a pair of sharp scissors. I imagined that with these invisible scissors she had severed Dr Rooknodien's lifeline. As you stood next to her, she seemed to hold them in your face. I made an effort to ignore them. I was more susceptible than usual because of Zebulon. I imagined that Maya, like Parker, was likely to know my secrets before I did.

I said, "I don't agree that Parker and I were ever as close as you are making out. Parker put up with me because of his trust in Solly."

"Parker was very critical of the Road Safety Council. I told Parker you are the one to take over Solly's role, someone to tell the truth. The alienation is a tragedy on both sides."

"What may have been so in the past becomes absurd carried too far forward. And, Maya, I am too old to be Parker's substitute for a son. As you also know, I have a son of my own who could stand some looking after."

"Is it as simple as that? You don't owe Parker a debt of gratitude for what he has done for you in the past, and up till today? You pick and choose your relationships, stop and start them however you choose?"

I said, "I don't owe anyone anything unless I choose to acknowledge that connection. Yes, it's so simple. Otherwise I am too far entangled with everybody who wants to tie a knot in my life. If someone can't choose to be alone, who would be able to write a taxi poem?"

I was moving away from these words even while they were

standing in the air. These sentiments were more sour than I wanted. I had contracted them in the course of half a life on the front seat of Parker's one Toyota. There was nobody like a sliding-door man to remember so exactly the injustices perpetrated against him.

I had too fierce a sense of the accounts that needed to be settled. Therefore I allowed all the others to slide away. If Parker had never been a true father to me, and Solly had never been an altogether true prophet, and Geromian had never composed his visionary taxi sonnets to reveal this corner of the world, and if Zebulon was not a true son and was carrying a gun around, then this was perhaps because I never asked them in a straightforward way.

"You don't sound right in the mind, my old friend, to say such a thing about your morality. You don't sound as if you can remember where you came from, how little you were. I don't hold it against you. I know what Solly meant to you."

"Oh, Maya, I should listen to myself first before I open my mouth. If I could say that something definite was behind Solly's death, that it was the Road Safety Council, or whatever it was, then I could truly tell the tale of Solly Greenfields."

I couldn't decipher Maya's expression. It was as if she caught me in a lie or some misrepresentation. I couldn't see this misrepresentation for myself.

This troubled me. I had the sense, even from those days, that Maya liked to catch people. You could say that she had developed a type of beauty queen's sadism. It was perhaps the result of wanting to look back at the people who were always looking at you.

"How's your son anyway? Zebulon, right? I hear that he wants to enter the transport sector, be a factor in the industry like his father. Parker told me. I hope you didn't encourage him. It's not the industry to enter at the bottom floor. Those years are gone."

"I don't want to discourage him either, not to the extreme. Otherwise he will take it on just to spite me."

"You can send him to me. I will look after him on behalf of his father, whom I admired then, and continue to admire."

"Everybody seems to want my son," I said. "In all frankness, Maya, I am not sure you would benefit him. He needs more normality in his life, one of the things I never provided, besides not being rich. I can't find him. He called me in the morning and then vanished. I am left in the position of begging his friends for information about him."

"Send him to me and I will be able to tell you where he is at any moment. I installed a radio in every taxi, even though it cost me a packet."

"A radio in every car? No chance of a sliding-door man falling off the radar for ten minutes? The times really are changing."

Here was another offer I couldn't refuse from another leading member of the Taxi Owners Association. I couldn't see how to answer. Maya wasn't the guardian I would select. Helena would be better, bad as she was, bad as it was that she had a plan as to how things were supposed to unfold.

It wasn't written into the stars that Zeb should become a sliding-door man. No astrologer read it there and published the facts in the *Daily Voice*. I was humiliated in front of Maya, and Parker, and Geromian. With this new son who had appeared in recent months and who gave me his packages to hold, with this new nettling piece of my old flesh roving the world outside my surveillance, I felt naked. I felt the shame of it spreading into my neck and shoulders. Soon they would know that he carried a gun.

Maya put her polished, buffed, middle-aged woman's hand on my arm. It burned there very slowly, like a dry-ice flame. She didn't have a wedding band but she did have a ring on her long beauty queen's finger. It was implanted with a thick piece of gypsy's jade.

In that jade, I was sure, Maya could see my future. Inside her ring was the green smoke of all my futures. She could blow it into any form that she preferred, as with Dr Rooknodien. I wished that I could blow it back into her eyes. I was so close to her, for a minute, that I could see the spots of black ink in her eyes. I was reminded of the gold fountain pen that our old headmaster kept on his desk and which he would empty and fill, empty and refill, in his purplish-black bottle of ink as he threatened you.

I believed I could write Solly Greenfields' great taxi poem in this very ink. If Maya allowed me I would dip my pen into her eyes and finish the last line before midnight.

"I have something to say to you, Adam, my old friend from school. Beware. The storm is closing around you. You antagonised Montalban already with the limericks you wrote about his mother. You have that negative charisma with people who don't have a deep reason to like you. Before you came back onto the scene, I warned Solly that his experiments with the Road Safety Council would do him no good. I take pride in making good predictions. I need it to run the company, as a woman. And I see a storm in your future."

"If you know something, tell me. Otherwise, Maya, I don't share your prophetic abilities."

Maya was wrong. Montalban, Parker's henchman, started a fight with me. Like everybody he paid lip service to the project of taxi poetry. But he had no sympathy with what the project entailed, which was, first and foremost, the existence of taxi poets. He didn't appreciate the attitudes, and whatever freedom I had to play the clown, or the fool, in Parker's presence.

So if, in the past, I made up more than one limerick about Montalban's habits, and his goatlike beard, and his goaty boyfriends, and his mother's boyfriends, and if these same limericks happened to have been memorised by one or more sliding-door men, and if they had also been overheard by Montalban himself, and if Montalban held a grudge tight to his chest, then that was neither here nor there. Why did Maya care? It had nothing to do with her.

Nonetheless, Maya was bad-tempered, as if I had missed some proposal that she was putting to me. She classified me as her old friend from school, and in a way it was true and she believed it, but I couldn't say that she was speaking truly. Her personality, like her hands, had the touch of dry ice.

For the same reason she was not necessarily popular with her labour force, the drivers and sliding-door men and transport poets. She was quick to give people the impression that she didn't like them. I had this same impression, and she didn't care to correct it.

Yet there was a period in the history of the world when I could even have been in love with Maya. I wasn't completely sure if this period lay securely in the past, when we had been at school together, or in the green smoke of the present and future.

But she was already gone and standing next to Phil Chuboso. Parker brought us into the dining room. I had a chair at the bottom of the long table, opposite Rosenstein.

At first, the conversation was about Solly Greenfields and his funeral. I didn't have anything to add. They complained much longer about the rising petrol price and the new Parliamentary initiative to regulate the transport sector, formalising the arrangements between the municipality and the Taxi Owners Association, which had up to now rested on a gentleman's agreement. A government commission would auction the taxi routes and pick-up locations to the operators.

The meal interested me more than business and bureaucratic talk. There was a restaurant stew from Habib's full of apricots, beef, cinnamon, and vinegar, which Parker plopped onto the plates from a heavy antique tureen. I inspected it carefully when it reached me at the bottom of the table. The stew looked like thick brown marmalade on the blue porcelain plate. Somehow it didn't have a smell unless you went very close to the bowl, whereupon it rose into your nose like Bovril.

There was even a snoek. It was presented whole in the Brazilian style, sliced length-wise on a rippled blue plate, in an embalming fluid consisting primarily of vinegar. Its shrewd wine-black eyes gazed out of the window, past the pink-and-yellow trees and the burned-out Toyota chassis which sat in its silver ash in Parker's garden under the lunchtime sky, in the direction of the pastel-walled changing huts and then the open sea by Muizenberg. I couldn't blame a snoek for dreaming.

Parker kept me until the members of the Taxi Owners Association retired. I was starting to worry about what he had to tell me. However, my conscience was clear. It was as clear as a taxi poet's could be when he was judged guilty in the eyes of the gods and he had a gun on his person. Did it help to be innocent? You could deal with the guilty but what were you supposed to do with the innocent?

"Come to my office. I got the builder to put it above the garage. So not everything is exactly as it was before. You're surprised? Even in the transport sector things are moving. Just to keep up, I need to use a computer and a fax machine."

The office contained a desk, two heavy black telephones, the computer, printer, fax machine, and signed prints of some of Solly's transport poems.

Parker was somnolent in social situations, but there was a demonic energy to his commercial life. I could imagine him punching the numbers on the telephone and assailing the unfortunate employee on the other end, hunting and pecking the number keys on his computer as he added figures to a spreadsheet, counting the notes in his moneybox over and over again, reading the offerings of his company's taxi poets, and stroking his mole. That was happiness. There were exactly as many kinds of happiness as there were models of taxis.

I was on my guard. I resisted Parker as I had resisted the school principal who had suspended me for bringing a top to class and reading Bukharin in chapel. In that case I wanted to escape the education he was going to administer. It had been the start of my many difficulties with authority, which, as Solly taught me to see, amounted to an objection to the way in which the world had been organised. The school principal always had something to tell you, some trinket of Lucky Packet wisdom. I tried my best to keep the vibrations of any such wisdom out of my own compositions but occasionally I heard the sound of that dog-eyed principal's voice in a line which came out against expectation.

Ten years later, I was back in Parker's office and wondering if he was going to take out a steel-nosed cane from one of the drawers in his desk and start fondling it, as my old principal had done in lieu of his wife.

Parker was more obscure than those cane fondlers, however. He sat next to the desk and didn't say anything for a minute, trying to find the words, stroking the same mole. Even in the sitting position he was asthmatic because of his weight.

Suddenly, and in contradiction of his vitality earlier that day, Parker seemed like a man who had suffered a stroke while he was waiting for the sentences to come to him. I had done something to him, made some invisible cut with the sword I wished to put down. His face hung there, much longer than it could naturally be, as if it was a cut of meat placed on a hook, stretched by its own weight and unchanging in expression.

I worried Parker was going to die there in front of me, beside the fax machine, which was inhaling a slice of paper and chattering.

Whereas I wasn't ready for him to go. Our relationship was a burden I wasn't entirely prepared to relinquish. I had defined myself against him and against Montalban and Geromian for too long. I would have been as lost without them as I was already lost without Solly. I didn't have a single person to tell about my discovery.

"I'm glad you put aside your objections and came to the house. Now you found the way back I hope that we see more of you. I saw you talking to Maya. Isn't she still so lovely?"

I said, "Just as beautiful as she was on the day Dr Rooknodien died. Have you noticed that she's beautiful any way you look at her and in any light? I don't want to say who it is that has the power to give you that kind of a gift."

"Nothing's changed, my old acquaintance. You search for trouble with everybody."

"Maybe. Today I have enough trouble on my hands."

Parker wasn't displeased. He admired a sense of humour, or at least something equivalent to Solly's feeling for the rueful and ridiculous and reversible side of life. Parker just didn't have the time to develop one himself. He seemed so close to death, even further towards the boundary than Marmalade, that I was afraid to make him laugh.

"I have a favour to ask, as you must have guessed when I asked you to come. I know you are responsible for Geromian while he's over here. Well, I would like Geromian and me to have a proper conversation. He can collaborate with the Association on a memorial to Solly. We should take some pride in our history. And I have some business on the side to discuss with him. Can you organise such a meeting?"

"I'll put it to him. But I can't promise anything. He's a tricky soul."

I didn't mind introducing the two men. They might act on

each other like matter and antimatter. Parker drew nearer to me so that, from beneath his silk shirt, I sensed his strange odour, which I had never noticed before, as if a mortician helped him get dressed in the morning. Things were changing, even for Parker. I had been stupid to believe that, in my absence, the transport sector would continue as before. I felt that my former employer was about to devour me, along with the snoek which had been lying on the sideboard in a ruffled porcelain dish under a cloth net.

Parker was suddenly larger. He rose around me and occupied the entire room. There was some strange and bewildering joy in his lopsided face. And I thought that, in some underground place, my life had started to slide without my knowing it. I wasn't letting things slide, as I did at the Perreira Institute when I was overwhelmed by the poetry of forms and memos, but it was happening anyway, as if an avalanche was beginning.

"Like you, Adam, I should love Solly. I protected him through my good offices at the Owners Association, despite the nonsense he started with the Road Safety Council. You remember that every year, on Boxing Day, Solly would write a taxi poem about all the motorway deaths since Rose Sunday. From all his imaginative creations I found that one quite macabre. But he didn't listen to my criticisms. He was not the type to listen to anybody. Nevertheless, I should always love and trust Solly on account of his great spirit."

I said, "With Solly gone, Parker, there is nobody whom I would want to know my heart."

"And if we had the opportunity to punish those who were responsible, if we can be sure about who was to blame, then we should seek justice. You go along with me?"

"I am with you hundred percent. Solly believed in the right of self-defence. He could be very fierce when he found an individual crossing onto his property. He was not the man to overlook an injustice, whether it was against the working class, or against his own person."

I couldn't tell if Parker had a point. But he generally had a game afoot. And his game was Monopoly.

One of Parker's night-time taxis set me down on Buitenkant Street as it made the return trip to Parliament side. Everybody seemed to have gone inside. That part of town was almost deserted apart from some men in religious white caps who were arguing on the stairs of the internet café.

I went past them and the shuttered Chinese supermarket. One of the owners stood outside, adding numbers on a solar calculator as if he was checking the result of an experiment. Yet there was no sun. Between the supermarket and the shop for mattresses there were a number of beggars who had already gone to sleep. Inside their thick blankets they could have been old men or children.

To my surprise, around the corner, the windows of my apartment were television blue, rising and falling in intensity as if the television set was breathing. Zeb was the only person who had a key, besides myself and Solly, and the only person I knew who took a keen interest in my television set.

Oh, Zebulon, and Zebulon, and forever Zebulon! In some part of my heart I feared that the Wednesday would come and I would never see him again. He had such difficulty returning a telephone call. I couldn't wait to hear his explanation before I determined exactly what he had given me that happened to have the same shape as a revolver. There were laws against murder and robbery but no law to compel a son to dial his father's number and explain his life.

Unlike Solly, I was protected by a security guard. He was asleep in his cubicle beside the gate. There was an electric heater by his feet. The hot air rippled up the plastic screen in front of the cubicle.

Argus Panoptes, security guard of the Olympian gods, had one hundred eyes so that many of them would be on the lookout while the others slept. The guard at my building wasn't so scrupulous, preferring to keep both eyes closed. He was more concerned about what he would see in his stereoscopic dreams. One day, I promised myself, when I was something more than a minor functionary at the Perreira Institute, I would reside in a magnificent building. It would have a guard who kept two eyes open.

I pressed the buzzer. The guard came out of the cubicle, as brightly and immediately as if he had never been asleep, and opened the gate.

"My son, Zebulon, he's up there?"

"He came a little while ago. He's grown big. You are very fortunate to have a son like that. Later he can take over from you."

"I don't know if I want that, for Zeb to take over from me. I'm not sure I have anything that he could even take over, except a certain attitude, and I don't know if I want to pass it on."

He said, "But that is what everybody wants."

"I think everybody wants different things. Over there, where you come from, a son takes over his father's cattle. Over here, a son can break his father's heart."

It was an impossible debate to settle. The guard locked the gate behind me, steadying the padlock. His belt was full of keys. I wondered how anyone could manage so many keys.

The security guard had worked at the building for seven months, yet I had never thought to enquire into the terms of his existence.

That was how much I had changed for the worse since I arrived at the Perreira Institute. As a taxi poet, you would want to talk to everybody who crossed your path, like the electrician soldering behind the building, or the mountain man who was washing his

143

trousers in Molteno reservoir in a mattress of soapy bubbles, or the hairdresser in her thirties with red nails who went to Clubland and weighed down her head with earrings, or the man with a breathing tube on the taxi and, behind him, the truant in his private-school blazer bound for Newlands to see the test match.

Solly taught me to carry on a conversation with the most un-expected creatures, just because God made the world in code and distributed the keys to this code according to no obvious scheme of intellectual merit or birth or riches or occupation or level of conspicuous piety. You sought them out from all these different hands.

On my way up the stairs I wondered if Zeb had brought any of his friends along. My son was an unusual creature, not a bird of a feather, but not so much of a loner either. I wasn't sure if he even had close friends, apart from Antonia.

In Clubland, from what I had seen of Zeb's behaviour and heard and inferred, my son was friendly but distant to all parties, the same way he imposed distance between his father and himself. Zeb was a neutral, a Switzerland of the heart, and prepared to take deposits from any Clubland party. I was sure that one of these deposits was the item in my backpack.

When I opened the door, Zeb was looking in the cupboard in the hall. He brought his head out as if I had surprised him.

"Hello, Zebulon. You looking for something? I didn't expect to see you here but it's a good surprise. I've been waiting for you to telephone back all day."

"I had some things to do. And I had a lot to think about."

"I'm sure you did," I said. I didn't want to give him the packet back until I was sure what was inside it, so I didn't mention its existence. "I'm just getting back from a meeting of the Taxi Owners Association. It's quite a week. I haven't had a minute to think, to be a human being, one reason I am so delighted to see you. Can you stay for a while?"

"I can stay for an hour. I have something to ask you."

"That's even better. I'll make tea for us. Do you want to put the television off meanwhile? I don't want you to starve. There are enough people on this continent who don't have enough to eat."

It wasn't exactly a joke. Nor was it received as one, nor would anything I said. Nowadays I was unable to make Zeb smile. Everything about me was an embarrassment, especially if I tried to have a sense of humour, or a personality, and in fact he seemed to like me the most when I was perfectly silent. I wasn't sure why anyone would want a statue for a parent. I went into the kitchen and sympathised with the mute leg of lamb at the bottom of the freezer. Its broth-brown skin was clouded with icicles.

Zeb didn't follow me. For my part I didn't want to get straight to the point. So what if he didn't want me to say anything? I kept him in the corner of my eye as I looked through the refrigerator, afraid he would disappear again. I didn't want to pry into his reason for coming until he brought it up himself. I wondered how long it would take to arrive at the package I had been carrying.

The television was still on in the other room but the volume had been turned down. It was Zeb's preference to have the picture on even when he was doing something else. I could hear him rifling through the drawers in the cabinet. I pretended that I couldn't.

After a few minutes, he came into the kitchen.

"So you've been busy? You were absent for Gil Etteh's class, not that he has anything meaningful to teach you."

"I had some things to do."

"What was it exactly that you had to do? Did it have anything to do with Antonia? She acted very strangely today when I ran into her. How's your work at the archive?"

Zeb looked impatient, and I shut up. The only person who had the advantage over me, in the entire cosmos, was my son, who also got to have the last word with me in every exchange, and he was totally unaware of the magnitude of his responsibility.

I conclude that irony is God's justice, and especially the burning plasma of taxi-poetical irony, its most concentrated and corrosive form, which is applied by and to us and which is so burning hot and so burning cold and so very acid and so very base in the very same moment.

I would never apply such an irony to my son, better it was on me than on him. I knew that he wanted me to ruin every conversation and, in the past year, I had done my best to oblige. My best was far too good.

In truth I found it difficult to be a parent. It was a knot I couldn't easily untie for myself. And it took more, today, to bring up a child. In the Stone Age, I guess, you needed only the stones. The information age was different. Each time Zebulon arrived it required an infrastructure to keep him going: the five thousand channels of gaudy television to which I now subscribed, a cupboard filled with silver bags of microwave popcorn, and an Orelhão cordless telephone on which he could make his various assignations. I hadn't needed much more than money for bohr and White Rabbits, plus taxi fare on the weekends and enough to pay for tickets to the Bruce Lee double feature at the Cockney-family bioscope.

Maybe there wasn't some point Zeb had to make. Sometimes, and more so recently, whether it was a positive or negative connection between us didn't matter. The point was the connection itself. And a negative connection felt more real, I guess, to Zeb, maybe because friction was a sign of heat, and heat was heat whether it was generated by love, annoyance, or hatred. He wanted to be somehow hot and cold with me at one and the same moment.

"Will you tell me what's going on, Zeb? You don't normally

come around here in the evenings like this, not during the week. I'd also like to know if, as your father, there is something I should know, some way I can help. All I want is to be of use."

"Nothing's going on. Look, just give me back the packet I gave you to keep and I'll get going. It's better if you stay out of the whole thing."

"I'm going to keep your packet until you voluntarily tell me what's going on with you. I won't give it to you."

"Then don't. You are always questioning what I say, and forcing me to question it. You think being a human being is just about giving out questions to people and it's your duty to be the examiner. You promised if I came to you, you would help me in whatever way I asked. I need to borrow some money. But give me the packet back."

"I will give you whatever you require, Zeb, in addition to what I gave you yesterday. I don't think you need to have this packet. And, if I'm going to help you properly, you're going to have to explain to me why you have it in your possession."

"The way you can help me is not to ask questions. About the money, I will pay you back."

"Then that's not good enough."

What question did I have for my son? I would have liked to know why Zeb didn't smile at me and yet smiled at everybody else. What question did I have for myself? Why was I so suddenly angry with my son and only with him and his flat style of talking to me?

But I wasn't up to it. I was exhausted after one minute of a confrontation. I was sure that if he knew of his effect on me, he wouldn't have the heart to be so implacable.

It would be enough for the telephone to ring and the hand in front of Zeb's face would go away. It could even be a crank caller and Zeb would be more than equable. Thus my son talked to a perfect stranger on the other end of the line with perfect abandon but when he came to me he talked sideways again.

I wanted to howl in his face and break the black plastic receiver on his treacherous head. So much love! So much pleasure in the other person! So much good cheer! So much openness my son Zeb offered to a Clubland friend, here today and gone to Plumstead tomorrow, so little could he muster for a father who is his forever! So easy and natural with everyone else, including his mother, and yet as uncomfortable with me as if I'd planted ants in his bed.

"You haven't condescended to exchange a word with me about dropping out. I can't allow you to give up your life before it's hardly started, young man. Meantime you expect me to say nothing. It's inhuman."

"I don't have to live the second life that you promised to yourself. You used up your own life. If you don't want to help me with this, then admit it and I'll go."

I said, "We don't have to rehash our arguments about your future. Just give me a word of explanation."

"I can't explain anything to you. I have to go anyway. Keep it if you want."

Zeb picked up his own backpack and left me, for the thousandth time. I saw tears in his eyes. I ran after him, down the stairs, although he was already past the security guard and in the road. I would have tucked my fortune into his nylon backpack and returned his packet without ever being sure what was in it. But if I did, I would never get another word of explanation out of him. To prevent this future, it was worth denying him some quantity of money today. So I came back upstairs and counted over my anxieties like an old woman numbering the hundred beads on her tasbih. I still had the packet.

PROBLEM #5: Where Zeb was concerned, I had only myself to blame. It was my fault how his thoughts were entangled in the taxi industry. From an early age I had told him my stories, carefully selected from my experiences in Parker's company, which should rightfully have chilled his blood.

As a parent I miscalculated. There was a glamour inherent to a narrative which differed from the thing's reality. It was like the halo around the electric light on the balcony. Just because some circumstance turned up in a story, from his father, it interested Zeb.

So I hadn't cooled his blood, but quite the opposite. I had turned his head unwittingly, as his mother accused me of doing. Zeb was precocious. He knew the minutiae of the companies, the differences between long-range and municipal operators, the make-up of the regional taxi owners association and the different politics between the factions. The people whose stories he was familiar with were the black-eyed, black-belt Gatesville girls, and the drivers, and the taxi poets and their feline companions, and all the captains of the transport industry I enumerated to him.

So for Zeb, the transport sector was the natural place to be when he grew up. Not just that, it was the only place to be, the adult equivalent of Clubland where everybody was a potential friend and every second person was carrying the pills.

On the top of the staircase, looking at Zeb's head and his thin shoulders as he retreated, I had almost wanted to leap on him and stifle him, wait until I stopped his heartbeat, and most of all his tears, and could be sure that he would never be unhappy. And, for just a minute there, it excited me that my desires should run so dark.

I went onto the balcony to forget my wishes. You could see all across the city from my suburb of Gardens. The mountain was already dark and retired. Between the side of Table Mountain and the crooked back of Lion's Head the evening star shone and sang through the violet haze. Later, if the moon put in an appearance,

I would watch the circle of torches around the mountain as hikers went about the crown.

If nothing significant was created in Cape Town, except for a certain quantity of transport poetry, it was because the city was devoted to female beauty, and cheap drinks, and dancing music, and French restaurants with outdoor tables, and convertibles, and old and new mansions. Yet, for most of the time, despite the things it refused to do and all that it refused to see, the city retained some indefinable property called good magic. It was only good magic which would save Zeb and me from the contents of my backpack.

The telephone rang. It was Geromian, who sounded sober. His voice was trembling ever so slightly. I was still angry with him for being alive.

"Pudding, I do believe that I'm dying."

"That can't be possible," I said. "You're as healthy as a horse. Besides, this is no time to die."

"My heart is not what it used to be. It sends messages to me about mortality. I haven't been well since I lost my suitcase. It just arrived and I may have taken one pill too many."

"We're all dying, Gerome. We don't get to say yes or no to it. It's the disease of self-pity you're suffering from. I imagine it's the other side of being famous. You never got used to the idea that being a person means having limits."

"Why do you say this now when I'm in pain? You're too hard on me, Ace, and one day someone will follow the same course against you. You didn't take my call this morning. Instead I ended up with Helena Bechman's doctor, who makes Helena look timid. Listen, I called you because you're the only person I trust in this town. As for the rest of them, it was a conscious decision to leave them behind. Let me say something to surprise you. In your desire to question and overturn everything, including common sense, I recognise myself. Will you save me tonight?"

"I'll think about it. Otherwise, take another one of whatever you've been taking. In fact take two of them. If we're both still alive, we'll see each other in the morning."

I was sure Geromian just wanted somebody to talk to at the end of an evening. While I was on the telephone I opened my backpack and put Zeb's Pick n Pay packet on the table. I promised not to look.

So I promised my friend Zebulon, my beloved Zebulon. I promised. However, to quote a Jerusalem Prime Minister, I hadn't promised to keep my promises.

So I opened it, and unfolded the brown-paper parcel at the bottom. It had been securely wrapped and taped, Zeb's handiwork. As I removed each layer of brown paper it became more and more clear that I was holding in my hands something that had the exact shape of a revolver. I left the last piece of wrapping paper around whatever it was that my son had given me to hold on the steps of the Pepper Club. Someone had indeed gone to a good deal of trouble to make it look like a gun.

THURSDAY

~

IF I MISSED six in seven parts of my son's life, like Solly who never saw Marmalade's fighting life, but only the nicks and scratches he received, then I was fortunate to see so much. Most of the time, apart from the Institute, Zeb was lost to me. I simply had to hope that the other cats treated him well.

At twelve or thirteen, he was capable of rainstorms and atomic sunshine. He showed such sudden torrents of feeling—laughter, and anger, and tears, and tears of frustration which came out at the corners of his eyes like needles.

This new Zebulon was different. He was cagey about his feelings. When he was frustrated I could tell by the way he lifted his hands and turned the corner of his mouth as if he was dog-earing a page. I noticed his hands stiffening, and a tremor in his Adam's apple, as if there was some subtle machine in operation.

Even when he was angriest or happiest or trembling with

righteousness against authority, he wasn't irrational. With the exception of his father he remained connected to other people. Not only would he never have picked up a gun to shoot someone, he could never have been as callous towards Geromian as I had been. Moreover I had been callous with an easy heart.

To think this, and that I had never cared to generate a surplus of love for who needed it most, returned me to the telephone which was ringing into my easy heart. I picked up the receiver and tried to decipher the voice on the other side. It was the bellhop at the Mount Nelson, Kamal. He was the one who helped to install the ionising machine in Geromian's room. At first I couldn't place him at all. It was ridiculous that he should be calling me when I had something that looked like a gun. The one thing didn't go with the other.

"I have been calling your number for half an hour, on Mr Geromian's behalf," he said. "The line was busy, and busy, and busy. I am almost worn out with dialling."

"I was trying to track someone down. Are you sure you have the right number?"

"No, you are the one I was told to contact since I could not reach the doctor at home. If anything happens to Mr Geromian because of me, I could even begin to hate myself."

"I'm not overly worried. Geromian was fine yesterday despite travelling so far. He needed to sleep."

"Now he has pain in his chest, and complains of dizziness. I sat next to his bed for an hour but he refused to let me call a different doctor because he didn't want to be charged twice for the same illness. In my presence, he took a number of pills from the suitcase which just came from the airline. Someone who cares about him should visit and make sure."

"I agree, Kamal. I am just not sure that you are talking to that person. I have other things to worry about. It's not a heart attack.

Geromian would be too much in pain to carry on a discussion. He would have noticed some amount of tightness in his left arm. If not, it's probably not his heart. Maybe it's a kidney stone."

"He said you were a taxi poet before. Since when, may I ask respectfully, do you have a medical opinion?"

"I have first-aid training because of the Road Safety Council, thank you very much. Look, I want to be on the safe side. I'll be there soon."

"I am now the most relieved person in this hotel."

Kamal shouldn't have been so relieved. I wasn't in a rush to go there and satisfy his guest's hypochondria. Solly had been the same way, imagining all the aches and pains and broken bones and words which never hurt him and thinking that every cough and packet of brown spit, as dark as cough syrup, indicated tuberculosis.

It was the disposition of a taxi poet, a slave to imagination which could turn a freckle into a cancer, and roll a fish wrapped in newspaper on the lady's lap at the back of the Microbus into the grandest of creations.

Notable personages, like Parker, or Helena or Sebastian Bechman, would have raced to Geromian's side. Helena would fuss over her precious speaker as if she had a heart of her own. Instead, Geromian got me. Because of Zeb I was even less sympathetic than usual.

If I had been unwell, I would have wanted to keep any critic at a distance. Geromian did the opposite. He wanted me at the hotel and had made me his chaperone. He could not abide the existence of even one critic, someone who had not been won over to his cause and was therefore a defect in his fame and the ruin of his immortality.

So he needed my approval to cure his own fear of death. I would never offer him this cure. So I was nothing compared to Geromian. But I was a stubborn nothing, and I was stubborn in the name of Solly Greenfields. If the universe was just, the same people who installed him in their temple and had never noticed that their idol spoke nonsense for three decades should attend Geromian in his room above the pink courtyard of the Mount Nelson and mend the heart which he had broken by himself.

PROBLEM #6: Before saving Geromian from himself I had the gun to consider. Something might be heard if I held it close to my ear. It was reassuring to hold, snug, and almost warm to the touch.

The gun was silent on the question of its history, where it had been and what it had done, and how it had come to be in my son's possession. I brought it to my nose and detected the scent of oregano, the remainder of the gunpowder. I liked the heft of it. It had more authority than a pen.

Solly had a fear of guns. To chase away housebreakers he wielded a zebrawood walking stick. At any sound he would pick it up and prowl from window to window to check if anyone had climbed over the wall onto his property. He swung it at shoulder height. With my luck this week, I was holding the same gun which forced Solly to put down his walking stick forever. I didn't want to understand what Zeb would be doing with it but I was sure that was why he wanted my assistance.

There were some days, some Thursdays especially, when you made your own luck. It would be a lucky stroke, for example, if nobody ever traced this gun back to Zeb. I spread a dish towel on the table and cleaned the pistol, inch by inch. I placed a radiant-blue drop of ammonium Handy Andy in the barrel, according to a recommendation made years ago by Montalban.

I flushed out the nozzle under the tap and opened the chamber to make sure, for the second time, that there were no more bullets in the thing. I found one in the chamber which I took out and put in my pocket. It had an orange tip and a yellow body and

155

I could feel it next to my heart. Afterwards I dried the barrel. I felt luckier already.

Once it was done I opened the freezer and hid the gun beneath a packet of I&J frozen peas. I didn't know when I last opened the compartment, probably before I joined the Institute. In there was a tray holding a dozen rusty cubes, as if a tin man shed twelve tears. I couldn't even recognise the tray.

So I had a special type of amnesia, forgetfulness of the heart. If somebody had asked about my feelings on Monday or Tuesday or even this Wednesday, before Zeb's visit, I wouldn't have been able to say. I had just put something under the frozen peas and I had to reach in to see what it was again and it turned out to be something in the shape of a pistol.

Despite his broken heart I suspected that Geromian would live longer than any of us, including the Bechmans, and would be telling stories about us, and how we had broken his heart, on Friday evenings in São Paulo. So I didn't go straight to the hotel. Outside was a cod-liver-oil sky, and the possibility of rain in ten minutes or blazing sun. The city's fifteen-minute summers and winters and springs and autumns reminded me of Zebulon. I went back inside to get a scarf.

I hoped to meet my son accidentally on the way to the hotel. Despite Helena's plans, the only real things in a taxi poet's existence happened by accident. I found Whitman by accident, and Solly found me, and also, in a sense, Zebulon, my cuckoo Zebulon who shoved the contents of my life over the side of the nest upon his arrival. With this gun he had done the same thing again.

Just as I opened the door Zeb called back. His voice was strained, as it usually was late at night or early in the morning, when it wasn't tuned.

"Where are you? Give me an address and I'll come and fetch you right now. Parker can send a taxi."

He said, "I'm out, okay? There's something urgent I have to do. I'll meet you at Geromian's lecture. Everybody will be there."

"I don't know what is more urgent than the revolver I found."

"It's a pistol, no revolving chamber, therefore not a revolver. With your huge experience, that you reference all the time, you should be able to tell the difference. I'm not sorry it is with you. Otherwise it would have ended up with the wrong person."

"At least you think I'm the right person, Zeb. That's some kind of consolation. But I would still like to know what has been done with this gun. And what you expect me to do with it. I'm not an arms disposal unit."

I expected an apology, and even an explanation. Instead, Zeb turned my Thursday upside down. The question of what had become of the old Zeb was as difficult to pursue as what had happened to the brand-burning young Geromian who rode the trains around the Belgian Congo and never deviated from the Trotskyite line, flaming with new life and new languages and new feelings and new wisdoms.

"I have to go now. I'll find you after the lecture and explain to you about Solly Greenfields. I promised Antonia I would go with her to the Institute. She's meant to meet Geromian."

"This is way beyond someone taking the wrong-coloured pill. I will find you in town if I have to. What do you have to do with Solly? Does that have anything to do with Antonia? Are you in love with Antonia?"

"It's amazing that I'm not."

"I wouldn't mind if you were. Never mind. I am going to come and find you."

But Zeb was gone again. I was constant while everyone else was changing. I had the idea that any alterations in Geromian had something to do with age, and the corrosions of fame, and spiritual lassitude, and the fact that he travelled in a limousine through Rio de Janeiro, and that nobody, even Geromian, was blessed with an inexhaustible imagination. Then there was the case of my son to consider. There were other nineteen-year-olds who didn't bear arms.

I had never really made the connection between Solly and my son. I admired Solly who ran the Road Safety Council where Antonia worked while Zeb admired her. But they seemed to belong to different societies. Solly was never really interested in my son, who, in his opinion, took my attention away from the field. He was antithetical to families and children, nephews and nieces. Instead, he leaned towards the neighbourhoods of Woodstock and Observatory and their beggars and student drinkers and dogged adult drinkers and the geniuses on every corner and the obscenities offered wherever a Hi-Ace alighted. But none of that, his relations with the beggars and the drinkers and the mountain men who slept under the bridge, was the kind of naked and demeaning and dramatic connection a child created. Even Solly didn't have my problems.

On his side Zeb heard my stories about Solly Greenfields as a man, but, so far as I could tell, he was more concerned with developments in Clubland and with his career as a sliding-door man than with my old mentor. Not for the first time I was as supremely clever and as dismally stupid about human nature as only a taxi poet can be.

I set out to save Geromian but ever so slowly. I took the long way round through town and, maybe, in the direction of the Pepper Club. I went past the old familiar buildings—the Somali shop, the Labia Theatre which was once an embassy, and the new coffee shops which served café pingado and chinesa from a machine puffing and shaking like a locomotive.

There was a chain across the doors of the Pepper Club which I associated with the chain I saw one time on the shoulders of the old mayor, Jabulani, who christened Parker's first Toyota Quantum in front of City Hall. Through the club's windows I saw an amplifier stack and coloured lighting, switched on in the daytime, and a counter on which there stood a few brown plastic bottles of Schweppes.

It was an odd section of the city centre, almost deserted during the day, except for passing trucks and the apartments five floors up from the street where an invisible hand was busy pegging bed sheets out of the window. The engine of a van was running fiercely in a loading bay on the opposite side of the street. There didn't seem to be anybody at the wheel.

In the evening it was livelier with the clubgoers, dressed and undressed to the hilt, as well as the corner cafés which were becoming, in the fullness of time, internet cafés where nameless foreign men sat at the computers and telephones and tried to make difficult connections to Congo and Central African Republic and Chad, places where there were coups and revolutions and military dictatorships. They used those telephone cards where you scratched off the back to reveal the coupon number. After an hour of calling their nails were thick with the gold paint.

Zeb and his Clubland friends, the ones like Roy and Salima but never Antonia, socialised in the internet cafés before the clubs opened and in the interim before the revolution. They sometimes played cards around a table. Zeb wasn't visible in any of the café windows, which were spattered with rain. I thought that my heart would break along with Geromian, and Kamal the bellhop, and the men in the cafés whose telephone calls could never be completed. The slanting rain rolled up and was blown back from the mountain all the way to the ocean to reveal a dome of such white-gold sunshine, what Solly called God's paint.

I remembered that, in Solly's first sequence, which included a sonnet dedicated to each day of the week and which he composed in the night kitchen of the Mount Nelson, he defined Thursday as the day without obvious coincidences, when you were least likely to run across a beloved old face in the same Toyota or to find a lost key in the bottom of your pocket or to win at the roulette table at Grand West because you bet the same number as your birthday. So, going by Solly's rules, I couldn't dream of finding Zeb on a Thursday. Maybe Solly was right. But he also said on a Thursday you made your own luck.

I went past the municipal library, converted from an eighteenth-century barracks. Solly had been opposed to public libraries, government libraries, because he said they only contained what the government wanted you to read. Solly had very occasionally revealed a sense of humour. I only picked it up in retrospect. Even then I was never certain that I understood the point he wanted to make.

So Solly was a funny man without being funny, a beautiful man devoid of any beauty. Could you say the same for Geromian?

The Mount Nelson had a story as grand as the white arches which guarded the entrance on Orange Street, and as extravagant as the pink terrace on which had dined many dictators and actresses and Trotskyite trade unionists and presidents of the Taxi Owners Association.

I knew there was also an underground history of the hotel connected to the taxi-poetry movement. Solly once worked as a cook, late nights, in the room-service kitchen in the cellar of the main building and composed a kind of lyric in honour of the dumbwaiter on which china trays and slices of toast and small dishes of gooseberry jam disappeared into the ceiling.

Geromian, as a man on the run, had stayed at the Mount Nelson, and had insisted that the management move him into the same large suite he occupied now. This demand, which may or may not have been communicated to the Security Branch by the hotel management, had resulted in his apprehension and eventual expulsion to Gorée Island and then his long exile in São Paulo.

The bellhop, Kamal, found me when I was losing my way in the Nellie's foyer. He had straw-white hair, although he was a young man, and, by some coincidence, a scarecrow's face and broomsticks for legs underneath his scarlet trousers. I was sure he had trouble with the birds.

"I can't tell you how pleased I am you could come, even if it is not exactly on time. Nonetheless it will do wonders for Mr Geromian's spirits. I couldn't have continued here at the hotel, in good conscience, if some harm came to him."

"You take your job very seriously."

"I believe that I do. Which is not to say that here is where I want to end up. I am interested in the same field as you and Mr Geromian. I spoke to him. He's agreed to consider a selection from my work to see if it has promise. I hope to persuade you to do the same. I feel that I have something inside me which needs to come out. I believe that I have the ability to accomplish something meaningful in the world."

"It's not a meaningless position you have now. This is a famous hotel in transport history. Solly Greenfields worked here. If I'm not mistaken, his sonnet sequence on the working week was completed here in the kitchen."

"I didn't know that."

"It's a true fact. Ah, but we don't care to remember our own history. We would rather know what was happening in Brazil and Mozambique and Angola at the same time than what transpired right here, whether it was Solly or the Bukharin circles. We don't even remember that it was this same hotel which saw the foundation of the Golden Arrow Bus Service, owned by the trade unions instead of the old capitalist formation."

I wasn't sure if Kamal even knew who or what I was talking about. He concentrated far too much on his bearing rather than the clutch engaging his ears with his brain. He had gold piping on the shoulders of his tunic and wore his uniform with military pride. He could have been the leader of an army of scarecrows.

I was escorted to Geromian's room. In the lift, Kamal occupied my ear with his unhappiness. He had composed a sonnet in honour of the Toyota Quantum which, by virtue of its engine capacity, was making the Hi-Ace obsolete. He wondered if I could find it in my heart to look it over. The subject put me off. The Quantum was a good piece of Toyota engineering, a big square vehicle with bucket seats and good mileage and a durable engine. Never, though, would it jolt you like a Hi-Ace flat-out on the approach to King William's Town where the mountains were God's most unanticipated choices from his palette, such oranges and yellows.

Kamal unlocked the door and I went in. Geromian was placed against the headboard with the blanket over his shoulders. I couldn't tell the condition of his heart but his head was so big as to constitute an affront. He was spread out on his back with his eyes closed, as if he was meditating. I couldn't bring myself to stifle him.

Nothing else would kill him. Geromian was strict about the chemical compounds entering his body. He could tolerate no grains nor margarine, nor one percent milk, the taste of which he compared to the breast-milk he had once drunk on Zaire Route 1, and, of course, no bad electricity. The legend had it that the truckers on Route 1 all made it to be centenarians. Geromian followed their superstitions and restrictions on diet, sex, and exercise. If he didn't live forever, he would be around long enough to see the completion of his pyramid in the collective memory of humanity.

Kamal went out. The click of the door woke the patient. I was disturbed to see how broadly he smiled at me.

"If your heart has been troubling you, Gerome, why didn't you call Helena's doctor or another doctor or an ambulance? Kamal would have been happy for the rest of his life, believing he saved you."

"I have a dread of doctors, as you know, Adam. You don't understand because you refuse to sympathise. This unique life force is something given to me to protect. Thus I automatically go in the opposite direction when they want to put me in the hospital. Helena Bechman is the danger. She wants to put my soul in prison, as she already did to you. Do you know that, after I came out of detention, and even after she accepted Sebastian's proposal, your famous Helena was convinced I was in love with her?"

"I wouldn't build Helena up into anything more than she is— an intelligent bureaucrat who wants to run the world according to rules which don't apply. I came voluntarily to the hotel. You didn't have to force Kamal to get me here."

"That fellow is so pitiful he's beautiful. Yesterday he presented me with a printout of his taxi poetry. People think I can read and absorb their absurdities. It's one of the blessings which come to me on the side, along with you, of course, Pudding."

"Can you afford irony in the shape you're in?"

"Not about you. I do feel blessed, however, as I decided last night when I was waiting for my heart to stop. Despite my heart I have had blessings showered on me. Not without good cause, mind you."

I said, "It's a good way to feel, to be blessed. I mean, I've been lucky about some things, of course, but I don't feel that way overall. I survived by accident."

Geromian was indeed blessed, by some inexplicable god who had perhaps cared for his father the judge, and conferred his protection on the son. Despite himself, Geromian had the Midas touch of turning a stranger into a friend. If this quality served him no better than it had King Midas, then it was perhaps for this same reason that his taxi poetry became popular. It spoke to you as a friend who wished only to share his love of the stars in the sky and the trucks on the road and the burning passions in his Brazilian soul.

Solly's taxi poems were different. They never stood waiting for you and only you, hoping to steal something from your heart on behalf of their creator. Solly's taxi poetry might sting you, or burn you around the heart, or switch from sweet to sour depending on where you placed them on your tongue, but never for a moment were they solicitous.

Geromian solicited the feelings of other persons. He needed you, in the plenitude of his vanity, and was open about it. It was a greater paradox than I could find in my heart to forgive. And I wasn't forgiven myself. He was going to tell me why.

"Ah, angel, you could have turned up an hour ago, if not for the sake of my heart then out of respect to an elderly man. Maybe you aren't as friendly as I thought. I said you have a friendly face. That's different to a friendly spirit. That is the one thing you cannot afford. I was thinking about myself a good deal last night, when I was sure I was going to die, and I decided you are mistaken."

"That's a surprise."

"You start from the premise that I cannot attain self-consciousness. If that were true, what kind of taxi poet could I be? On the contrary, I don't trust blindly in my own words. The thought has occurred to me that this ceremony is a fraud, along with all the people who now want to celebrate my career. Where were they all along? Of course I don't trust them and their so-called Institute. Maybe I never captured the spirit of the trans-Kalahari. It's not unthinkable, even for me, that my entire career is based on nothing."

"I didn't say that it was. And I wouldn't agree with the statement. There's a lot that's valuable in the history of transport poetry, including yours. Even your severest critic would say that. I am sure of it."

"Some at your university would say that transport poetry itself is based on nothing. You cannot dismiss me, captain, because I am not the same as Solly. Not even he could manage to be Solly Greenfields. I am only surprised your hero worship didn't kill him before. And please, don't give me an explanation. Clever as you are, an explanation costs you nothing. I would say to you what I have said to everyone in the field: if you can't be loving then don't speak a word. When you have turned over every stone in search of a justification, taxi poetry is just another word for love. If you're not capable of it, then, by all means, retreat to an institute. See if they have found any substitute for love, which begins with myself, I grant you, but from there it goes out into every part of the world."

Geromian got up and wrapped a dressing gown around himself as he talked. He went to sit at the vanity table which had a central mirror and two on the sides so you could inspect a panorama of yourself in triplicate. He had turned the side mirrors so that they reflected each other to infinity.

I had no explanation to give. It sounded true that I had an unfriendly spirit behind a friendly manner. If Geromian had limited intelligence on himself, he was nevertheless shrewd about the twilight soul of another. And it was certainly true that I didn't love him as he required.

It was love's fault. This relish for monetary compensation, for hotel luxuries, for never being asked a difficult question, and, in general, this monstrous and bottomless desire always to be consoled and complimented and praised and lauded to the skies had nothing to do with his fear of death. The love instinct flourished unchecked. Now it had stifled every other part of his soul.

Maybe I was just the same except that, unlike Geromian, I could hardly stand to be loved and thus had never obtained followers of my own in the public or among the Perreira students. I wasn't desperate enough to be loved. Maybe the very essence of taxi poetry was frozen love. Maybe, also, there were too many of these maybes, a short word which took you anywhere.

I said, "Let's go back to the beginning. About this evening and the lecture, Gerome. It's irrelevant whether I have a friendly spirit. I think you should give the lecture. You have the chance to influence a generation of apprentice taxi poets, far more than Solly ever managed to reach. It's another way to have descendants, better descendants and admirers than your current bellhop and the other sycophants. Why do you continue in the field otherwise?"

"Can I ask you a favour? Shut your mouth for a minute, would you, and stand aside? My head is beginning to hurt again. Or it's my stomach tied in knots. Or it's my back. Sometimes I can't differentiate. I've had some difficult years, captain. I have to find the right tablet. Now that my suitcase is here I should be able to function. Then we can converse about your lecture."

I stood aside. Just as if he was a mad person, Geromian opened the small suitcase on the dressing table and began taking out bottles and packets of medicine, muttering while reading the script on them as if he was testing a line under his breath, frowning, and lining up the bottles one by one on the night stand to form an army of white-and-blue-capped toy soldiers.

As the army was assembled, it reminded me of the Chinese emperor's terracotta warriors, who accompanied the emperor into his grave. I didn't interfere. Geromian could do what he wanted with his tablets. I was sure Zeb adopted the same Swiss policy towards his associates in Clubland who were always carrying something in their pockets.

Some of the bottles were familiar from first aid: sleeping pills, blue tranquillisers, anxiolytics which took away your worries, large white vitamin capsules, as well as St John's wort and Rescue Remedy. I never saw so many pills before in one place, except on the shelves in Lunat's Pharmacy. Behind the edifice of Geromian was a chemist's shop filled with all these feelings, such self-hatred and self-love and self-protection, made concrete by these white and grey and green and yellow and dark-blue packets and bottles and paper trays of tablets and capsules. There was something to put him to sleep, something to wake him up, something to restore his faith, something to calm his nerves, even something to speed up his nerves, I was sure.

Solly had been more sceptical about medicine, except for his dentist, but he could also be anxious and hateful and detest himself and get the jitters if he was on the front bench of the taxi and could see how it was being driven, and he would come home and lie in the bathtub for six hours straight until his hands didn't tremble anymore.

So they were both hypochondriacs. Underneath Solly's armour, behind Geromian's edifice, I wondered now if they both hadn't disintegrated. When you dealt with them, what you generally got was nothing human, as such, nothing humane or connected, but instead the beautiful calm of the hysteric. There was an eel in this person. It looked out at me through the holes in his skull. After a minute I understood that it wanted me to do something.

"Get me something to drink this with, Adam."

I fetched a glass of water from the bathroom.

"Much appreciated. You have no idea how this changes the situation, these tablets. They make everything go away. If I come in ten feet of a hospital the medical establishment will bury me without giving me five minutes to catch my breath."

"Still, that's no reason for avoiding them."

He took three pills and sat down on the bed. I sat down beside him. I wanted to make peace because I had other problems. To my relief Geromian had also subsided.

"I didn't mean to scold you like that, Ace. My nerves will settle. It's the red pill that keeps me going in spite of the most draining circumstances, some kind of potassium compound. They say it's a placebo, just because I believe in it. But I have my doubts and if I have doubts, can it truly be a placebo?"

I said, "Take as many as you like. We need to have you in fighting shape."

"Maybe I'll have one more of these. Adam, you cannot put your faith in doctors and their ideas about dosages. A taxi poet cannot live according to the limits which other people prescribe. They will take your entire life away with limits."

"I can't say that I disagree. That's how I feel about the Perreira Institute. Solly was probably right that it would be better to burn it down and start from nothing."

Geromian took another tablet out of the bottle and swallowed it. He was improving before my eyes. It must have been that I had rescued Geromian from being alone with his heart, or that he was happy with his expensive hotel room, or that I had brought him water for his capsules, and there was a kind of Florence Nightingale effect. He wasn't angry for the delay in seeing to his broken heart. There was some different chord which had been touched in him. In anybody else I would have labelled it kindness. I didn't deserve it. I had a gun to dispose of.

What was I to Geromian? I was no more than the bellhop. I was a supplicant who talked above my railroad station and had composed taxi poems which circulated on taxis on which I scarcely set foot. He didn't bother to remember my crimes. Three minutes and any serious feeling Geromian held against me evaporated. It left nothing but a bright red tinge on his tongue. His feelings were like evaporating tears.

"I mentioned a favour or two, Gerome."

"If the pills allow me, I can do anything. They allow me to do everything. They even allow me not to hear your attempts at mockery. Shoot. What is the favour? Is it something to do with your son?"

"Nothing to do with Zeb. Firstly, I promised you would talk to the student protesters, as you know. There's a girl called Antonia, from Mocímboa da Praia, who's the big chief of the Perreira revolutionaries. Plus, Parker wants to meet with you. I wouldn't ordinarily ask but he was my employer. More importantly, he was a good friend to Solly, even after the Road Safety Council. He may simply be an admirer of your work."

"Given what you say, it's unlikely."

"I agree. I don't think that it's simple admiration on Parker's part. I couldn't tell you whether Parker is even capable of true appreciation, as opposed to his habitual manipulation. Apart from his friendship with Solly, he belongs to the old school in the taxi industry, when they had a very narrow understanding of culture. But something interesting may come of it for you."

Geromian agreed. Even if he had forgotten my transgression, however, I had to pay a price. It was required to restore the standing between us. And I paid this price with both my ears.

"On your request I will meet with your friend Parker, at a place and time of my choosing. In fact tell him to come to the hotel today. And Antonia, if she's attractive, bring her to the lecture.

However, I'm not finished with you. I was thinking, during what I thought was my heart attack, that you have an original intellect precisely because you started out as a driver, with no real ambitions. I want to tell you something about yourself. Do you want to know it?"

"I'm not sure that I do, Gerome. I don't think you're giving me the choice."

"Out of all the members of your generation, you had the trick of finding a new angle. And I believe you can thank your experience of starting at the very bottom for that. However I do not see you as a pioneer in the field. You are too quick with words, and your judgements, and whether you are capable of true seriousness remains to be seen. People can hear they are being mocked. That is something you don't understand, which I offer for your enlightenment. So we will see in the fullness of time, which is the answer to everything. And we will see what happens at the lecture this evening. I will be on the podium. Insha'Allah."

"As God wills."

There was something inspirational in Geromian's absurdity and atrocity, his epic self-admiration which extended to wonder at his own words, and his restless and mind-ridden energy fuelled by every red pill, and yes, despite my sensitivity to vibrations in the language, his absurd and armour-plated way of talking. I mean, who sounded like that?

When I left the presence of Geromian, just as with Solly, I was refreshed. Parker or Helena, on the other hand, drained you completely, as if they had just taken a blood donation without your noticing. Geromian made my blood sing, and whether this was a song of contempt, or a song of such sweet adoration, made no difference on this Thursday. Maybe it was this ability to fill the ears of another with hurdy-gurdy music that was the essence of being a taxi poet.

Thanks to the Thursday curse, I still hadn't managed to run into Zebulon. I had some hours to spare in which a coincidence might still happen. Antonia might have some knowledge of Zeb's existence. I had an idea that she would. Also, I wanted to apologise to her for myself and Helena Bechman. It was an uncomfortable position, as a transport poet, to be a counter-revolutionary. It put me on the same side as Montalban and Rosenstein and the conservative section of the Congress Party.

I went by the offices of the Road Safety Council. They were located on the second floor above a building-supply store and a men's tailor which made suits for export. There was no sign of Zeb among the half-dozen students keeping the organisation together. They hadn't seen Antonia either.

I wished that I had taken Zeb to Solly myself when there was the opportunity, to absorb his milieu of inexpensive but carefully chosen pleasures, from the chamomile tea, and sugared mebos, to the Parliament-Funkadelic records Solly placed voluptuously on the turntable. Yet the new Zebulon had better appointments.

I had nothing to turn my hands to. It was so odd to be free in the middle of the most difficult week of my life. When I thought about it, today was the first Thursday since I was fifteen years old, and an unlicensed driver on Lower Main Road in Observatory, when I had no reason to move it and get on and find something to do. I was careful to be busy to prevent my thoughts filling up with worries and mysteries. The world zigzagged at every opportunity. While an institute or a road safety council or a taxi owners association went in straight lines, the human heart was as crooked as ever.

Back at the flat I did housekeeping to keep my worries out of mind, spooning grey mincemeat into Marmalade's bowl. His cat's eyes wandered lazily, as he browsed in the bowl, over the birds on the balcony, starlings and warblers and grey tits. At least they interested him. It was a relief. You could see his curiosity, which was the same as the life force, in his orange fur.

I continued the snoek poem in my mind. It was Solly's taxi poem, which I never composed for his birthday many years ago and which I had managed never to compose every subsequent birthday. I had a long section in the middle which was in reasonable shape, including a comparison between the beauty of the Hi-Ace and the utilitarian virtues of the Microbus and how beauty was the secret form of usefulness.

Although I had some good ideas for the main body, the first line didn't come right. My mind was filled with tiny white bones.

I remembered how Solly Greenfields inserted the bulk of his fat hands into his mouth in search of snoek bones. He would continue talking to me while exploring the inside of his mouth, trying here and trying there to remove the source of his discomfort as if he was about to dislodge a tooth. Eventually he would get satisfaction, cough the bone right into his hand, and place it delicately on a saucer alongside the others he retrieved.

That was Solly's combination, which I could never convey to Zeb or any of my students, Solly's unique way of being fussy about the tea china into which he poured his chamomile, and the every lilt of his truck sonnets which sounded in the volta, the sonnet's turn, as if an axle was turning, and the priestly punctuality with which he attended to his cats, and his perpetually renewed nakedness in the bathtub, and the toothbrush hair in his nose and ears, and his toenails which seemed to have glazed in the kiln.

If Solly would never use a swear word, he could still sulk at you for a month for coming out with the wrong opinion on a taxi poem. He could talk for an hour about the shooting pain in his scrotum after wearing his too-tight pair of velvet trousers, the ones faded in the bottom, with threadbare white belt loops.

I thought the combination, the sweet and the sour, the ever so civilised versus the brusque, had something to do with the kind of place we were and our specific type of history. Solly wasn't dialectically necessary, contrary to the Bukharinites, but the fact of his existence gave a different feeling to history as it unfolded anyway.

It was no excuse for a man at his level, just in terms of taste, to wear velvet trousers. In them he looked like a half-gorgeous, fat-legged butterfly, another of what a Bukharinite would term as Solly's productive contradictions. I thought I would start my snoek poem with a dedication to Solly, its inspirer, in his velvet trousers and with a piece of fresh snoek melting the news wrapped around it.

I went up to the Perreira Institute, where I was irrelevant. Zeb was nowhere to be found. Somebody said that Geromian was on his way in the company of Parker. Sebastian Bechman was escorting members of a Brazilian foundation around the university. He was as handsome and friendly and untrustworthy as ever. The secretaries, both men and women, had their lunchboxes open in front of their computers.

The place was as busy as an anthill, and Helena was the ant queen. The worker ants were carting boxes out of her office down to the auditorium.

Helena went along with them. She took charge of the details on an important occasion. A technician ant was setting up the sound system, calibrating the volume, and running a cable across the side of the ant hall. The apprentice ants, in their trade-union dungarees, were moving folding chairs from the classrooms into the auditorium.

I didn't want to get caught doing nothing but worrying about Zeb. As Solly, or Geromian, would say, a taxi poet should incline to loafing and idling and following the absent moon. Yet, within the Institute, as administered by Helena, nothing could be more strongly disparaged than a moonlighting member of faculty. There was business to do in the sunshine.

Helena was too busy to notice my existence. The dignitaries were in attendance. There was a Petrobras limousine, with boxy looks, discharging various members of the Congress Party I should have recognised from the newspapers I didn't read.

Clubland was out in force—boys with staples in their ears and long, loose trousers, girls who might have been boys on account of their closely shaved heads and boots, and other girls who wore only leggings and T-shirts, and other boys and girls who had nothing but pills in their pockets. I wouldn't have guessed that any of them cared about a taxi poem other than the one they might have seen while hallucinating.

There were new currents in the world, new sources of electricity, new ways of creating sparks. So I failed Solly's test. I had lived long enough to see one revolutionary current succeeded by a second, and a third, and a fourth, and my sympathy with changes had run out.

To my surprise the sliding-door men had also turned out to hear Geromian. They were the new generation in the transport sector, not from the traditional recruiting grounds of Woodstock and the Bo-Kaap, Solly's territory, but from unheralded and unimagined locations like Rondebosch East, as far afield as Durbanville and Somerset West, and the rows of two-room RDP houses in Gugulethu.

Their women came in head scarves, heels, glitter, and tight Soviet jeans, Cape Town Cleopatras. Their main purpose seemed to be to insult their sliding boyfriends, as well as to keep them from talking to other women who looked just like them. They swore rapidly. I hoped Zeb would never fall in love with a sliding-door man's woman. For she would only allow you to fall back out of her eyes at a high cost.

The sliding women had fringes high on their foreheads, and long ebony hair straightened and cooked into a textile by a ghd. Their eyes were heavily pencilled. I knew that if you looked into them, it was more than possible that you would fall in. So maybe you shouldn't stand too close.

Instead of Zeb I found Helena. She detached herself from Jonas for a minute and came over to me, her elbows moving at her sides as if they were part of a steam engine, pumping up and down to turn the axle. Her complexion looked as rich as an oil painting.

I could even see, as she was about to run me down, why Sebastian, along with her graduate students, revered Helena so. She was used to solving problems, making decisions on behalf of other people and in the name of the greater good.

On Helena's efforts depended the functioning of the Perreira Institute, thus the minibus poetry movement, thus the quality of life for fifty million commuters. She had this bureaucratic weight on her shoulders which could never compete with the butterfly's mass of an individual taxi poem. Nevertheless, she would never survive a week of my problems. I didn't offer myself as rougher and tougher than anybody, including Helena, but I didn't see what right she had to be rougher and tougher than me.

All this railroad weight bore down on me in the foyer. I wanted to be crushed. If I did love Helena then this was my motivation. I would not describe it as masochistic, but rather as the tendency of the travelling soul, a taxi poet's soul, which moved inside at one hundred and eighty thousand miles per second, to associate itself with whatever has the greatest possible momentum.

"I have a bone to pick with you," she said. "We're supposed

175

to start and the guest of honour hasn't arrived. I just spoke with the hotel. They said Geromian had some kind of medical episode overnight. You encouraged him to take more tablets. Everybody knows Geromian has a problem with tablets."

"I don't know what everybody knows. I'm paid to have some idea about the other things, the ones that nobody knows. And I'm not being evasive, like everybody else at the university is. In this instance, really, Helena, I'm not the right target. Pick on somebody else."

"You can't expect me to decipher the code you talk in, Adam. I would have expected you to notify my doctor that there was a problem. He believed he was having a heart attack."

"Given enough time, all of us in the profession become hypochondriacs. Because we spend so much time listening to our minds, eavesdropping on them, we begin to hear all sorts of things which aren't there. Geromian will be fine."

For all the affection I wasted on her, I felt that Helena was waving me away. Maybe I was sensitive because of Zeb. An institute for taxi poetry shouldn't take such a practical view. For all we had to do with actual taxi poems, on the sides of actual Hi-Aces and Quantums, we could have been an instituto de cones do pinho, an institute of pine cones.

Maybe it would be better to study pine cones than minibuses. Nobody's heart would break on the scales of a cones do pinho and nobody would have to die in the back of a railway worker's living room in Woodstock. Solly's death wasn't Helena's problem. Taxis and guns and martyred men didn't belong to her lists of problems. I was the problem.

"I should also forget that you put Geromian in the company of a notorious taxi gangster like Parker? What kind of cockamamie idea was that? The reason the Perreira family supported the Institute was to separate the intellectual pursuit of transport poetry from the gangsterdom out there. You're putting that all in danger."

"So if it is not Geromian, it's Parker. Who do you suppose runs taxi world, Helena? If it's not Parker then it is people who are worse than Parker. Twenty years ago, who was Gerome and who did he hang around with in Zaire and Congo? He won't mind Parker who, after his own fashion, is a gentleman."

"I mind that you put my speaker at risk, along with the credibility of my Institute. Apart from Antonia, you have been nothing but a hindrance this week."

Houdini, if he had to deal with Helena Bechman, would never have escaped. Even tears weren't enough. I wanted to weep at her, not from love, but from frustration. And I wanted to sneeze. They were painful, powerful emotions, underneath the nails, and the pain they wrote in me was intricate and convoluted.

I could hardly breathe for it. There was some cruelty in her manner, some sparkling cruelty which flashed out as if I was turning a piece of crystal in the light. I had some strange passion to defy and then to submit to her cruelty. It was the only type of love that she could offer.

For Helena had no tolerance for error and approximation. She took your mistakes and built on them until their existence and their amplitude were the cornerstone of your relationship with her. I could almost believe that Sebastian never made a single mistake, and this reminded me that the Bechmans could not replace even one of the bus conductors whose sliding dialects they had studied at the University of Lisbon and who, unlike the Bechmans, made fresh and original mistakes every day.

Like my sliding brothers I was proud of my mistakes. They were the secret chromosomes of my existence. On the way to find a telephone and track down Geromian I decided that Helena should be the one to cry, my pine cone, Helena Bechman.

I used the telephone in my office to call the Mount Nelson. Kamal told me that Parker had indeed taken Geromian. He talked to me about his application for ten minutes while I kept an eye out. Zeb was nowhere to be seen from my window. Then I saw Parker and Maya and, thankfully, Geromian as well arriving in a long Parker's taxi and put the receiver down. I hurried out of the building to intercept them.

Maya had one hand on Parker's back and the other in Geromian's arm. She was taller than both men and made sure to stand on Parker's bad side, the one with the mole. I tried not to notice her brown silk dress, and her brown high heels, and her small high breasts, and her red lips.

I wondered whether a beauty queen was necessarily in the company of beasts. Maybe Maya made a fetish of Parker's mole and maybe she put her ear to it and listened to its rising and falling blood as she would listen to a seashell on Milton Beach. Once upon a time I was in love with Maya. It might have been today and it might have been tomorrow and it might have been ten years ago.

But I had a job to do. I could decide about Maya once I escorted Geromian. I had to separate him from his new friends. I put my hand on his shoulder and admired his linen jacket and lemon trousers. He could have stepped out of a clubhouse at the main station in colonial Kigali. In his absurdity he was beautiful. The same could be said for every line of taxi poetry he produced. It was for its absurdity that I had loved it although, like many other loves, I couldn't spell out the reason until I was disenchanted.

I said, "Gerome, for once I can truly say that I am happy to see you."

"You asked me to talk to Parker. I talked to him, and his Uruguayan friend. He wants me to make it clear what role Solly played in the history of taxi poetry. I have no problem with that, being naturally generous. In exchange, including my endorsement of his plans to negotiate with the government about the new routes, Parker is going to think about a sponsorship."

"Do you really need the money?"

"I don't have as much in the bank as you believe, Pudding. The minute you are successful everybody imagines you must be a millionaire. But how many millionaires are there in the field of taxi poetry? Only Charlotte Monaghan is what you could call rich and she got there, as you know, by borrowing without asking."

"I don't know anything about what Monaghan supposedly took from you. I could never see it with my own eyes but if you insist, I believe that every trick in her book is borrowed from you. And what is a book but a collection of tricks? Look, Helena is about to murder me. Can we tell her you're here?"

"Helena should learn patience. She had a hankering after me when she was still a student at the University of Lisbon, despite Sebastian, and wanted to arrange a session with the three of us. She has the idea that every man she meets is secretly in love with her. Actually, it's the other way around."

Geromian was back. There was no indication that yesterday his old-man's heart had wanted to stop like a broken wristwatch. He had gone all the way down and had come all the way back up in the course of twelve hours. Helena was wrong. The red pills did something to repair a heart. Maybe you could live forever on a diet of red pills.

I couldn't excuse myself to collar Zeb, who I had just seen at the back of the auditorium with Antonia. It was excruciating to be caught with Geromian instead and the business of the lecture. I would find my son afterwards and get the answers I deserved for having brought him into existence. Meanwhile there was a bullet in my pocket.

The hall was silent as Geromian began. He had written his talk on a series of notecards which he shuffled before our eyes and picked up at random. But they seemed to come out in a good order.

He started with the era of decolonisation and its importance for his own life. In the space between the old colonial regimes and revolutionary movements like the Congress Party, between the state and the guerrillas, the taxi companies arose. With them came the possibility of taxi poetry, and the chance for him to shatter the consciousness of Clarens, and to offer the sketch of a better society where one person wasn't doomed to be in the driver's seat while the other was meant to be driven around.

There was electricity in Geromian today, as there was once in Solly Greenfields, the kind which only circulated in a big-enough field. Five hundred people in the audience, from the bus drivers to the university administrators, crackled as he explained how he decolonised himself from his father the magistrate and all his many fathers and mothers, how this narrow frame of reference had been replaced by the domain of the Portuguese language, which stretched from Brazil in the west to Macau and Malacca on the other side.

In the newly independent states, about the same time Solly was travelling on the municipal bus to Mowbray to cash in his coupons, Geromian mixed with people of all climates and adherents of all the revolutionary ideologies. He hid in safe houses owned by Lebanese traders and Somali merchants, slept with black and brown and white men and women, boys and girls, combined the accents of Portuguese Angola and Mozambique, and Tswana, mountain Sotho, truck driver's Dutch, and a thousand dialects never remembered to paper.

So what if it wasn't harmonious? If it wasn't immediately beautiful in the simple-minded sense? Taxi poetry was not a matter of the beautification of commercial trucks and buses. Beauty was regressive if it merely accommodated working people to the existing conditions. Then it simply worked on the side of transportation capitalism. A taxi poem should have lines so jagged you could get a paper cut.

If I wasn't so disturbed about Zeb I would have wanted the speech to be more logical. Thanks to the red pill, perhaps, everything in this electrifying discourse, all Geromian's sense and nonsense, was mixed up with everything else—the absurd and the astonishing, the clichés and anti-clichés, the earthy and grandiose, the cosmic and New Age philosophy, politics and madness, the historical details of the taxi poetry movement and the trivialities of his self-absorption. I couldn't straighten it out in my thoughts exactly. I shouldn't expect to. A thought was just a watt of electricity, after all, and a second thought was a second watt.

Should Geromian make perfect sense? You shouldn't ask a taxi poet, who could propose a new image to the world, to advance a scientific doctrine. Solly was not so grandiose as Geromian on the surface, until you caught him singing songs from Donizetti in the bath, but he mingled just so many facts and human tendencies and mangled logic and heard, above the sound of his own voice, the rumble of just so many forms of traffic. It was a taxi poet's condition to belong to the undead and be forever suspended between the sun and the moon, between sugar and mustard, and, above all, between the clatter on the street and the melody he produced in each taxi poem, as if it was a music box which was also a Pandora's box.

I loved and hated Geromian on the podium. Everybody else simply loved him. In one beat of my heart I turned my hatred to the audience instead of the speaker—from the Congress Party officials who benefited from government tenders to the union-owned Golden Arrow Bus Service, the drivers and sliding-door men, the taxi scholars who chose this being as the supreme living expression of the field, and the others, from libraries and school departments and Trotskyite book stores, who followed Geromian as a prophet. In the name of which god did he speak?

As their sarcastic and quicksilver emissary from the heavens above, Geromian didn't neglect to criticise his audience. He cursed them for their middle-class values and their fear of the poverty which was the only nobility in life, and even the narrowness of their ears and tongues. He compared our Capetonian context to Rio, a city where everyday speech had a small beauty of its own, unlike our rough syllables. Here he found the same philistines as thirty years ago but without the excuse the previous generation had of living under a police state.

I should have remembered from before that Geromian was only too happy to talk like this, float beside his audience like a butterfly and then sting them like a bee. He was never happier than when he was denouncing somebody and preferably everybody. In a different context, he would have been a sultan who put his adversaries in burning oil, commissioning countless statues of himself while sending the opposition to re-education camps. It was a commonplace that the great taxi poets were the unacknowledged dictators of the world. What it really meant was that, in a parallel universe, they would have been real dictators.

This evening nobody would have to be re-educated. I saw five hundred shining faces. The audience had come to the Jose da Silva Perreira Institute for this very reason, and to be abused, to be scorned and denounced. It was the abuse of everything they held dear which demonstrated that they were getting the real deal. They would go home and live the same as before, but more electrically, still without allowing these impious thoughts to touch their existence.

I half expected Geromian to ignore Parker's request about commemorating Solly. I was half wrong. At the end of his presentation, after his final card had been turned over, Geromian talked about Solly's parallel career to his own. With surprising affection, he talked about Solly's long baths when he composed with a hand on one of his cats, his early contributions to the political consciousness of the taxi-poetry movement, his unyielding resistance to any kind of doctrine, even the Bukharinite and Trotskyite formulas, and his unerring ability to reproduce the sharps and flats of the Cape Town language. I hadn't expected Geromian to be so precise about Solly's virtues. He had some idea of what was truly great about Solly Greenfields. Maybe it was true, and maybe even Geromian had more than one façade.

I wondered what Solly himself would have said about it. Solly was better at avoiding unnecessary entanglements like the Institute and lectures which caused him physical pain to be in the audience. He would have been appalled by the praise. He would have stayed in his kitchen and, if anything, listened to the address on the radio.

Then Geromian trembled, and started coughing, and his eyes went so blank it was as if you would never see the bottom. I'd had the same impression on Tuesday, at the airport, and wondered if Geromian had been taking pills at the beginning of the week.

As we watched, the speaker swayed and held on to the podium with both hands. He was startlingly red in the face, not a natural shade for a human being. The audience was applauding so much that they hardly noticed when Geromian left the stage and fell into the chair next to me as if he had been chopped down. Somehow Zeb had found his way into the other chair next toAntonia.

We brought Geromian to the private room behind the auditorium. Helena helped him walk. His complexion was drained and grey, and he had his eyes closed. Then he opened them when we put his feet up on the chair. I took his shoes off and saw that his feet were horny.

"Pudding, do you think they got the idea? Do you think they understood, finally, what I've been trying to say all these years?"

"They all loved you, except me, and I am a hopeless case, as you know. The ambulance is on the way. Sebastian has already sent Gil to get hold of a doctor."

"I'm fine. Send everybody away. Just allow me to breathe. I just need air in my lungs. Don't force me to talk."

Geromian wasn't dying. I had no such luck. I let him fall back into the chair. He took another red pill out of his trousers and put it in his mouth. Another student and Helena and Sebastian Bechman stood around us until the patient got onto his feet and indicated that he wanted fresh air.

Antonia looked as if she had been slapped. I was sure it wasn't Zeb who had done it. She was in some trouble. If I was a responsible member of the Perreira Institute I would contact her family in Mocímboa da Praia. But I wasn't so responsible. Meanwhile Helena had a fierce look in her eyes, as if Geromian's condition was my fault. I forestalled her by moving towards the door.

I said, "Zeb, stay with him and Helena. He wants to talk to you in any event. I promised Antonia she would get to meet the great man. Just don't let him out of this chair. I am going to see about the ambulance."

I went through the auditorium, which was in chaos. People were going out and coming in and moving in all directions. But there was a kind of joy in it, as if a prophet had been sacrificed in front of us and on our behalf. I saw that Gil Etteh was on the telephone to the ambulance driver.

By the time I returned Geromian was pretending to be completely recovered. Somebody had wiped the perspiration from his forehead. I almost felt pity. His Thursday had been almost as difficult as mine and he must have liked the idea of being able to talk to interns and refusing to answer Helena's questions about his state of mind. And, even with his broken heart, he had to put up the illusion of being immortal.

He was leaning on Zeb. "I'm not a stranger to your family. As a matter of fact, Zebulon, I knew your father when he wasn't much older than you are today. He was driving one of Parker's Hi-Aces. Solly Greenfields was trying to educate him, making him read Yehuda Amichai, Whitman, Zbigniew Herbert's shorter pieces, others from Eastern Europe who opposed transport collectivisation. And I've heard things. People like to confide in me. I could tell you a lot of stories."

"My father wants me to stay in university and to be something sensible, like a railroad lawyer, or doctor. He didn't even want me to enter the Institute in the first place."

Zeb was never openly hostile to me. He wasn't sly, or under-handed in any way, and didn't have a combative bone in his body despite who his father was. On the other hand, he couldn't pass up a chance to embarrass a parent and this despite the fact that I had a revolver belonging to him in the icebox and we were standing with Helena and Geromian was leaning on his left shoulder.

"That doesn't surprise me, because your father reveres education, precisely because he has never really benefited from it, and doesn't see the inherent limitations. Now the jury is still out as to whether anyone has ever succeeded in teaching your father a single fact. And since you bring it up, whether it makes sense to teach a taxi poet his profession. In my time we had no such thing as institutes. Instead we had trucks and buses, motorcycles and motorboats. We absorbed our language straight from the people."

Give Geromian this. He was good at accepting admiration, even after too many red pills and a fainting attack. He made a point of returning attention to each person. He saw each individual,

I guess, even Zeb and Antonia, as an opportunity for further self-realisation. At least he saw individuals. But there was no more processing time to worry about Geromian. I had to find out more about the gun. I didn't want my son to be around Geromian for any longer than necessary.

I said, "Gerome, I may have to leave you for a few minutes. Zeb and I have something to discuss. You'll be well looked after. Meanwhile, whatever I say, Helena's going to insist on taking you to the hospital. The ambulance is coming for you."

"Not if I can prevent it. I also have constitutional rights."

"Nonetheless, someone should take a look at you tonight. The constitution only applies to living persons."

"In that case, leave me alone with Helena and Sebastian. I don't necessarily want to be treated as a patient. They will try and talk me into bed with them again if I show a hint of recovery."

It was confusing to look from Geromian, to Zebulon, and Antonia, and back to Geromian, and think that they could inhabit the same space. Solly Greenfields had once asked to meet my son, waiving for once his policy against the existence of families, and I had turned him down for fear of exactly this confusion.

"Antonia, will you stay with Geromian until the doctor decides what to do? Sebastian won't leave his side but I'd prefer to have someone I trust there as well."

"If you insist, I can stay with him. I've wanted the chance for years. We are meant to negotiate a statement together but he is not in the right shape."

"I insist you negotiate. If he is left alone with Helena and Sebastian Bechman his heart will freeze. And now I really have to spend ten minutes alone with Zebulon."

I excused the two of us as the private ambulance duly arrived at the gate, two red bars flashing along the top of the vehicle. I saw what Zeb was wearing for the first time. He was dressed in

186

a tattered pinstripe shirt which once upon a time had hung in my closet, plus a duckbill cap, and the old maroon suit jacket that he favoured already at Westerford, and the clumsy white shoes with bright red shoelaces which magnified his footprint until you could see nothing about him but red laces. There was nothing to distinguish my son from all the superfluous Clubland humanity who came and went and lived and died like taxi drivers. The thought pressed on my heart. Zeb could be an ambulance poet. He could fix your heart without taking out a blade.

"We need to have a conversation, young man, if I am ever going to keep my conscience as a father. Let's go somewhere private where we can talk until the ambulance goes past with Geromian. And while we're walking you can enlighten me on a point of interest. Where's the gun from?"

I hadn't expected Zeb to answer. I had hardly seen him through a chink in the wall since he'd become an adult. But I saw immediately that I was expecting too much of him to keep up the effort of building and rebuilding this wall. He looked as if he wanted to fall down. Maybe his week had been worse than mine.

"It's not mine. Somebody only asked me to keep it. They couldn't take the risk of keeping it. I was only trying to help a friend out, as you've told me many times to do."

"That's what you have to tell me? You were trying to help out a friend? And you're saying I told you to help out your friends? I told you to stay away from your friends, not to make them my friends."

"I won't lie to you. I wanted you to help me by keeping the gun. Where is it now? I can take it back now. You can wash your hands of it. That's what you always want to do."

"It's in my fridge," I said, "underneath a bag of frozen peas. I always told you to stay away from guns, Zebulon. They don't bring good news to anyone. And as a taxi poet, if you have one, you point it at yourself as a matter of principle. I just don't want to talk now in front of all of these people."

"There's nothing to be ashamed of. You'll hear the story and you will know that there is nothing to be ashamed of."

"There's always a reason to be ashamed. Let's find our way back to town. I'm sure Geromian's heart is fine and he is up to his usual melodrama. I don't know that I even want to say goodbye to him."

We went past the entrance to the university, and then down to Rondebosch Main Road. There was life late into the evening: the video shop which didn't close and sold microwave popcorn and cigarettes and had a pink light on its awning, the corner cafés beset by young men and women socialising without seeming to need anything from the shelves, and the chicken-burger shop, and the frozen yogurt business which was miraculously still open, revealing the young man behind the counter scattering nuts into his pans of vanilla and chocolate. The taxis were moving in the direction of town, heading for the chip-and-polony shops, the late-night Congolese cafés which sold smoking black sausages off the brazier, and the Clubland discos.

Also miraculous, on the third floor of one of the apartment buildings, was a girl in a backless salmon-pink dress tight on her thin brown arms, who stepped out magically onto a cinderblock balcony, a cinderblock Cinderella earnestly adjusting her make-up in the mirror on the back of a compact, entirely unconscious of the people on the road just below.

She couldn't have been older than Zeb. And I thought about other parents, and their other children, with a kind of longing and jealousy which could never be felt. You could never truly be jealous of someone's child. I was only jealous, I suppose, of someone's easiness with their children. Nothing had ever been easy for me. Everything I did seemed to have been tied in a knot by God beforehand.

For some mysterious reason the middle-aged Solly Greenfields had taken an interest in me. The same concern hadn't passed from me to my son. Solly had asked to be introduced to Zeb, true. Otherwise he'd barely acknowledged Zeb's existence, or the fact that I had any kind of personal life apart from taxi world.

As the author of Zeb's existence—for all authors are jealous that others love what they create—I never quite came to terms with this fact about Solly's personality. I could never predict to whom or what Solly would be indifferent.

I looked at Zeb beside me. "I had no idea you were working for the Road Safety Council. Now, Zeb, you turn up with a gun. You put a gun in my hands and don't bother to explain. For all I know, it is the same gun which killed Solly last week."

"It is the same gun. I was there when Solly was killed."

It was midnight. And then it was Friday.

FRIDAY, SATURDAY, SUNDAY

~

I HAD six or seven problems. Who was counting? Zeb dealt with everybody's problems in Clubland. His friends wore him out. The only person who didn't take too many pills and wasn't saving for an abortion was Antonia. At the Institute, Antonia was recognised as a leader among the revolutionary students when Zeb enrolled. But nobody else in Cape Town knew her name. She was in a hurry to change that.

So she was in a hurry to change everything. Compared to her, the rest of us were slow. In my seminar she had composed more than one taxi poem off the top of her head, as if she was whirling a top on the table between us. Nobody could do that except Geromian in the old days. If she struck you as brittle, and you noticed that she was impatient and didn't like to be contradicted and wouldn't delete so much as a semicolon when you questioned its existence, then it only went to prove the magnitude of her talent.

It was a paradox. She wanted everything to change, yet she didn't let go of anything. I saw that she couldn't let go of anything on paper or in person, any sensation or disturbance or accusation or vibration she picked up in the back of the taxi. Maybe it meant she would be the next Charlotte Monaghan.

Antonia was too serious for Zeb's other friends and for Clubland. She was isolated, one reason she relied on Zeb and Solly. For this same reason she took on too many responsibilities. She had day-to-day responsibility for the Road Safety Council. When the hostel closed, over the long holidays, she moved into Solly's lounge where she slept on the couch. There had been weeks when they spent all their time together, almost like lovers, and went around to Dom Pedro's or Coleridge Road Café to talk and drink until the doors closed at two in the morning. Zeb, as he told me, often found them together there.

In the context of Mocímboa da Praia, where the Portuguese language brought a more open-minded attitude, it wasn't unusual for an ardent young woman and a much older man to pursue a conversation until two, as Solly and Antonia did, ranging from Bukharin to García Lorca to Pessoa, and the fado queen Amália Rodrigues, and Cesária Évora. In a place like Mocímboa the Chirindzas might have tolerated and even encouraged Solly Greenfields to educate their daughter in this fashion. They might have sent her out with their blessings and a basket of limes for her friend. Antonia's father might have struck up a relationship with Solly and brought him back to the house.

The Chirindzas might even have taken some pride in the revolutionary and intellectual credentials of their daughter's companion. But they would have known when to draw the line.

Meanwhile in Cape Town, with our doggerel civilisation, nobody respected the lines. What caused Solly's death was that he

191

never saw a line he didn't want to step across, and maybe that was because he didn't speak a language in which drawing a fine line was an art on the same level as taxi poetry.

I blamed myself for what Zeb told me when we got home, far more than I could blame Solly and his need to push the limits. I was the person who glamorised taxi world, and made a hero out of Solly Greenfields, and a mug out of Geromian. I made it seem as if there was nothing more interesting.

Zeb was the main beneficiary of my imagination. I had deceived him with my Friday's tales, taxi tales which were hardly false and hardly true, and which I told purely to entertain him. I had told him about Parker, Geromian, Montalban and about the war between the long-distance taxis and the municipal companies in 1995. I left Parker's service after the driver right beside me was shot in the throat. I had never been good with a gun. Neither were Solly and Geromian. It may be that keeping a pen in your hand ruins your ability to handle a gun.

I never counted on Zeb taking my stories about the taxi industry so seriously. But he had a lot to tell me about their influence. When he cycled along the Rondebosch canal with Antonia and she took him to meet Solly, it was like meeting a man from a legend. Then this legendary man put a pinch of cat mint in a dish towel. He let Zeb and Antonia watch Marmalade roll frantically over it and under it and around it until he subsided all of a heap with stupid eyes.

On the same day, Solly played a record from his extensive collection of bird songs. Marmalade's ears pricked up, first the healthy one and then the tattered one. He sprang onto the speaker cabinet from where he considered the invisible hadedahs, hoopoes, plovers, and snipes. Ten minutes went by. Finally Solly lifted the needle on the record player, releasing Marmalade from his enchantment. The cat was rewarded with a string of raw purple livers from a Pick n Pay container. He ate them as quickly as if he was drinking water and then hid under the couch.

That first evening Solly had been particularly interested in Zeb. He didn't mention his parentage but it was clear that he knew who Zebulon was. Solly was sharp like that. He didn't miss the psychological side of life just because he took a cosmic view. He must have thought that he could steal my son from me. Zeb sensed that I had in some way offended Solly, even if he couldn't put into words the nature of my supposed offence.

On other occasions Solly was distant, as if Zeb had offended him in his own capacity. Antonia started to take Zeb along to the poky offices of the Road Safety Council, across from the 24-hour Mowbray Mobil. You couldn't say no to Antonia when she descended on you and made it seem that there was nothing more important to the future of the working classes than walking her along the overpass, past the firehouse and the cement blocks around Hospital Bend, until she could unlock the security door that had protected the office since it was firebombed the previous year.

Upstairs they would run into a sweating old man called Solly Greenfields, who had nothing in common with the retired taxi poet of Woodstock, cursing at the budget figures and insisting on doing Antonia's calculations over although he invariably failed to carry a digit and never came to the same answer twice. Around Solly nothing added up properly. He was something of a nuisance as far as the operation of the Road Safety Council was concerned. While Antonia had a member of the provincial traffic department on the line and was trying to negotiate on some aspect of policy, Solly was smoking cigarettes with the window washer, lying on his back in the middle of the platform, and borrowing change from the interns for lunch money. Then he went into action. He practised his special breed of magic on the photocopier, which shivered into action and then broke down precisely three minutes after Solly lumbered out the door.

In all his behaviour, there was little trace of the legend Zeb had heard about from me, neither in the way Solly talked nor in the content of his conversation. If Geromian had been diminished by success, it was possible that the same had happened to Solly for the opposite reason. I don't mean to say he was a failure in anything but the world's terms. In his taxi poems, each like a seashell, you heard the sounds of another world, an ideal one in which taxi poets were honoured and where the lady at Woodstock Public Library, across from the Kentucky Chicken, was more familiar with Greenfields the transport poet than the other Greenfields, who ran the discount clothing store in Salt River. There were mermaids in those seashells of Solly's, flying on the foam, but you found salt water in your ears.

To be sure, Solly never talked about disappointment. It was possible to argue, as Zeb did, that I had contracted disappointment on his behalf. I made knots out of my life. In my corner of the Jose da Silva Perreira Institute, opposite from the cold-drink machine where people queued up during the day, I tied a knot in the red tape which came my way and sent it back to the administration. I would have had something to say to Rapunzel if she'd wandered into the stairwell beside my office. I would have had something to do with her hair.

Zebulon, on the other hand, puzzled through a complication until he completely straightened it out. As a boy, he laboured for hours to organise his collections of Lego bricks and plastic soldiers and the curved tracks remaining from a train set. He didn't get up until they were sorted and packed in their crates. Solly was a complication in Zeb's life, somebody he wanted to understand, although he obviously wasn't in good condition. His hearing had

194

deteriorated. Zeb found Solly's electric bell clapping in its bronze housing without him so much as noticing the racket. Marmalade also took leave of his senses. The cat was deaf, dumb, and once, in obvious distress, urinated in the middle of the living room. Zeb mopped it up.

Solly was stubborn. He only heard what he wanted to hear. If he and his cat had trouble hearing, it was because the universe was suddenly soft-spoken. He refused to accept that an animal was ready to go. As I saw in the past, when he found his companion stretched out cold beside his bed in the morning, Solly paid a visit to the charity pound in Woodstock that same afternoon. It was the best thing that could happen. You heard the rejuvenating effect in every syllable he composed after the arrival of a new animal.

Solly was finally as old as his oldest pet and it was more difficult than ever to say what he loved apart from animals and the comfort of political opinions unaltered since the Revolution of Carnations. Maybe he had run out of love. I never figured him out. He had been as much a legend for me as for Zebulon and nobody can approach a legend in his mind. There was the strange way in which Solly talked to people on the train to Simon's Town, where he went to paint on public holidays, and the stylists at the Barberton hair salon who gave him a discount because there wasn't so much to cut, and the ushers who let him stay in the back of the Gatesville bioscope between the end of the one double feature and the beginning of the next. Then there was Antonia.

One evening, not so very long ago, Antonia stayed at Solly's place to finish some work for the Road Safety Council. She dealt with the new bill on transportation in front of Parliament, which proposed to transfer the functions of the Taxi Owners Association to a public commission. It was raining so hard that Solly set dishes here and there to catch the water streaming into the house. Marmalade disappeared with such weather. Antonia or Zeb, if he had been there, would take a stepladder and find him on the top shelf of the cupboard, next to the mains, content to sit on an old blanket in the dark with the heavy scent of shoe polish around, like a chicken brooding on her eggs.

If Zeb had been there, he might have seen the strange look in Solly's countenance as he leaned over Antonia's shoulder to correct her spelling. He might have noticed that Solly came through the kitchen once and twice and a third time to see Antonia and offer his usual opinions on snoek, and kwaito music, and the decline of transport socialism in the 1980s, and a thousand other topics unrelated to whatever was in his mind. You could define a taxi poet as the person who finds it the most difficult to express what is on his mind. Instead of saying anything about that, Solly put on his Dollar Brand and Billie Holiday and Lead Belly records and took them off again halfway through the song as if he couldn't bear for the music to finish.

If you didn't know that Solly cared far more for humanity than for specific individuals you might have suspected that he was in love with a particular person for the first time in his life. Geromian had the advantage of always having been in love with himself, whereas Solly had only been in love with the cause of taxi poetry. So he didn't know how to sort out this strange new excitement. And Antonia didn't know that it would have been better to return to the student dormitory than to stay under the same roof as Solly. Maybe she even wanted him to fall in love with her, as she wanted everybody to do, and hadn't thought about the consequences.

To cool down, Solly ran his usual bath, which in this case was half rusty tap water and half rain water pouring from the roof. Once the bath was running you could hardly see the outline of his heavy body amidst the steam and the water and the soap.

Solly moved, from time to time, in order to lay himself differently along the tub, which had a fine network of lines in its porcelain surface as if it was an old painting. He must have lain there, with his old heart beating under the water, and dreamed about Antonia in the next room. She was much younger than him, and from a different world, but nothing had ever been accomplished in the field of taxi poetry by respecting boundaries.

Besides, Solly must have wanted to be touched. He must have yearned for it. He wanted to avoid death forever. His feelings had been growing inside him and wanted to be expressed in songs and caresses and dancing and everything else he had denied himself for the greater good of taxi poetry and its revolution in language. If he had a better memory for his own verse he would have remembered how he said somewhere that the most dangerous person in the world is the one who is making up for lost time, because time and loss are forever increasing.

Antonia came to the side of the bath when he called her. She hadn't noticed Solly's look, as if his lucky star was shining on him, or the way he studied her while she typed the documents for the Road Safety Council, or the way he came into the kitchen and trailed his hand on her back as he read over her shoulder. Antonia stood and talked to him, smiling at his eccentricity, and averting her eyes from his bulk in all the cloudy water and steam and rain and heat. Solly got her to sit on the side of the bath. For a few minutes he must have talked simply to keep her there, in a giddy way which nobody ever heard out of him under normal circumstances.

Without any warning he rose out of the water and put his arms around her. He kissed her neck, which everybody said was long and beautiful, and buried his snout between her breasts, as if he had wanted to be there for a thousand years. Then he tore her blouse, trying to take it off, and forced her halfway into the tub beside him.

As she was pulled in Antonia thought she would drown underneath him. She pushed him, and screamed, and cried, and begged him to let go of her, but in some language that he didn't understand. Finally she hit Solly in the face so hard that there was blood in his mouth. Then she hit him again, got out of the bath, slipped back in, and finally rose out of it, leaving only her dignity in the water. She locked the bathroom door from outside and went to fetch her suitcase from the lounge. She thought she could still hear Solly crying in the tub, although soon he got out and began knocking on the door.

Antonia went to stay in the office of the Road Safety Council. She couldn't bear to return to the Institute, where she would simply be another student with a predictable story. Nor did she communicate with Zeb, or anybody else. She had bruises where Solly had taken her by the arm and even more bruises on the inside, given that she had relied on Solly for his attention and admiration. He had taken the better part of her Cape Town life away. Antonia, the revolutionary, had her own specific love and hatred of older men. She wanted to banish the memory of his unexpectedly strong hands and even more so, the possibility that in a corner of her travelling soul, she'd invited it to happen. In one of Solly's taxi poems, composed years before Antonia ever came to his door, he compared the line of hair from a young woman's navel to a gunpowder trail. For Antonia it had begun to burn.

Solly called the Road Safety Council, but she refused to speak to him. He came to the office in Mowbray where she didn't allow him past the security gate. He brought her a tower of red carnations, imagining that he was courting her, but in the end he had to push them between the bars. In other words Solly hadn't learned anything from the experience and maybe it was the same stubbornness in sticking to his beliefs and to what he saw before him that fed into his writing.

It might have still added up to nothing, and evaporated with nothing more than hurt feelings on either side, if Antonia hadn't finally given him the chance to apologise. She had gone over to his place last Saturday afternoon with a gun in her pocket to protect herself. If Antonia knew anything about human nature, she would have known that you would need much more than a gun to get an apology out of Solly. He never said sorry to a single person in his life. He thought Antonia was arriving to apologise to him and give him a second chance. And maybe I idealised Solly and it went to his head so much he thought he couldn't be wrong. Maybe it was even my fault, which was the fault of believing that a taxi poet was a proper object of reverence.

It didn't take two minutes to end the life of the grandest taxi poet in existence. Antonia rang his bell and agreed to come in. Solly could be so persuasive, his being pleased to see you written on his jowly old-man's countenance, that you even thought he was going to say sorry. He removed the battery from the bell and put it in again. Looking along the barricaded cottages and the back wall of the Chinese shop where there was a stack of shipping material, he might also have wondered whether his electric bell was ringing in his favour.

When Solly followed Antonia into the house, he put his arm around her waist and kissed her neck, ignoring what she wanted to say, as if he was forgiving her for their lovers' quarrel. He tried to take her back to the bath where the water was running loudly. The gun went off. It went off again, and again, four more times, until Solly changed his mind and decided that his lucky star had been no more fortunate for him than the rabbit's feet and foam dice which the sliding-door men tied to the mirrors of their Hi-Aces and that his blood was thicker and blacker around him than seemed natural and that he had perhaps forgotten how to draw another breath.

If you knew more than Solly Greenfields about electricity between people, you would have predicted that the next thing Antonia did was to walk into Murray's corner café with spots of blood on her arms, as calm as if nothing unusual had happened that Saturday, and took out her change so she could summon the one person who was likely to lend her a helping hand. She had been mugged the week before and had lost her cellphone, while Zeb refused to carry his around.

Nevertheless Zeb managed to be on the other side of the telephone when he could never be around for me. She didn't tell him what it was about, but he came anyway on a Parker's taxi in twenty minutes. He went in first and found Solly lying in the middle of the lounge. There were polka dots on the wall which, when you leaned in to check, turned out to be blood. The gun was lying on the telephone table where Antonia had abandoned it on her way out.

As Zeb picked up the gun and put it in his pocket, the telephone began to ring. He backed away from it, saw that Antonia was almost white-lipped in horror, and decided this was a scene out of a Friday's tale and that he knew exactly what to do. Hadn't he been trained by my stories? He disconnected the phone cord, removed the tape in the answering machine, and set out a bowl of milk for the cat, who stood suspiciously on top of the dresser in the bedroom, prepared to fight. He saw that the bath was full to overflowing and considered pulling the plug, to let the water out, but then he didn't. He went around packing Antonia's possessions in her suitcase. She settled on the couch and didn't move or say anything while Zeb tidied the house. Finally she took the dressing gown from the peg in the bedroom and put it around Solly's shoulders. Together, without speaking, they wrestled the body onto the couch and placed a blanket over him. Solly looked peacefully away when Zeb closed his eyelids.

Then they did their best to get out of the house without being noticed by the neighbours or the men who hung around for hours half inside the doors of Murray's tea room waiting for a backgammon game to begin. Yet, the sliding-door man in the Hi-Ace had already noticed Zeb. He told his employer, Parker, when the news came out about Solly's death on Sunday morning. The sliding-door men were Parker's spies all around Cape Town. I should have guessed that he understood more and I understood less about the situation.

At Solly's funeral, Parker already knew some of the basic facts about Zeb and Antonia and Solly's death. Maya must have also known. That was a story for Monday and when it was told I hoped it would finally cure my son of the need to help anybody and everybody who knew the sound of his name and with whom, by the way, he wasn't in love.

I wanted to straighten the world out before I let Zebulon out the door. When he was inside my flat he was safe. It was only when he went through the door that he ended up in Clubland and underworld Cape Town and helping a dead man, who happened to be my oldest friend in the world, onto the couch. I called the hospital. Geromian was alive and well but Antonia had vanished. I had to keep Zeb here as long as possible until I found her. It would help if he went to sleep. And I didn't mind the idea of closing my eyes for five minutes and dreaming of a way to get everybody out. But it would only be a dream.

"You have any idea where Antonia might have gone? Does she have any friends besides you? I would have insisted that she come with us, after the lecture, if I had any conception of what you just told me."

"She wouldn't have come. Antonia doesn't trust you."

I asked, "What do you mean?"

"No, she thought you were blackmailing her over the boycott, and that I told you what happened at Solly's house. I couldn't convince her otherwise. She has the idea of going to Maya Rooknodien, where she did her internship. I was going to go with her. Antonia needs a witness. Otherwise the taxi companies will kill her."

"Even I don't want that to happen. We judge people by their actions. She dragged you in. She knew you liked her, and used that to try to get out of the consequences of her actions. And I cannot sympathise with the fact that she took this gun to see Solly Greenfields. Where was that necessary?"

"You don't understand. The gun was for her own protection, considering the types of threats she got at the Road Safety Council from people like your friend Parker. Solly was such a saint in your eyes. But even when he knew who I was, he never had a good word to say about you. He was always trying to win the students away from the Institute and to run it down, even though you gave him the reputation as the true spirit of taxi poetry. He wanted to take Antonia and everybody else away from you."

"It seems like a discussion we can come back to. He was probably tired of being a father. Maybe you should stay here, Zebulon. Let me deal with this before it becomes more of a problem. Then you can return to the Institute."

"I think I have to go."

But he didn't get up from the couch. I wondered if Zeb would go to sleep automatically if I closed the windows. As a boy, he did a tour of inspection of the entire flat at night, pulling on the door handles and the latches on the windows to see they were properly closed, and looking in the cupboards in case they contained ghosts. Only after his rounds would Zeb go to sleep, which he did as instantly as if you'd put him off at the switch. This time I did it for him. I pulled down the blinds, shutting out the train yards and bus depots and the necklace of streetlights across the shoulder of the mountain and the old brick apartment building with a mournful naked bulb on each landing that bore witness to something in the lives of all the inhabitants. I still couldn't imagine how Zeb had thought it was a good idea to move Solly's body.

Solly Greenfields never believed in families. Instead he had cats and baths and a lacquered music box which produced a spare rendition of flute-and-harp music. I didn't know where it had gone. And I remembered counting the leopard-brown and black spots on his neck and shoulders. Up close, if you came upon him at his bath or just out of it, he had a smell of raisins and prunes and baking soda. That was the sweet and sour of it, the snoek in Solly's heart, whereas my son, whose beauty was as measureless as all the coins in the pockets of every sliding-door man, was sweet, never sour, but obscure, as if the fish was in my head.

Zeb was my kryptonite. Around him my unfriendly spirit lost all its power. It reminded you that a taxi poet's irony, which did overturn colonial regimes, could be itself upended. There had been many nights Zeb wouldn't remember when I got in bed beside him; his steady heat, and breathing as regular as a cuckoo clock, and ceaselessly fluttering cuckoo life, reconciled me to another day as a sliding-door man. I would even say that Solly had wanted Antonia near him for a reason which might not be any different. Or else he was more stupid than I realised.

"I shouldn't have built up Solly as a hero in the real world," I said. "He was a hero of the moving word, which is different. All the same I cannot understand the rules you live by, Zebulon. What do you owe a person like Antonia Chirindza, who has nothing but ambition to justify her existence? Oh, I admire her cold-bloodedness and I can see how you can mistake admiration for love. But I lost such a father in him, and I never had a proper father. I am not suggesting he was blameless. I can't tell what demon got into Solly, except his whole life's story. Nobody ever loved him properly. He was isolated at the centre of his taxi poetry. Not even I should love him properly. I almost abandoned him these past few years, but only because I was caught up by the Perreira Institute."

Nobody was listening, as I discovered. Despite himself Zeb had fallen asleep on the sofa. I settled a blanket over him and couldn't find any sign of anxiety in his face. He didn't feel the harm of having a storytelling father. Meanwhile Marmalade had come out, purring as furiously as if he was a musical instrument and some unknown hand was plucking his strings. Before I knew it I was also asleep and Marmalade was under my feet.

I worried in my dreams about Zeb's falling almost in love with Antonia. She shot a man who had been Parker's friend since they went to the Chinese shop together. Once he had the gun, which was the only proof anybody besides him could ever find, I couldn't imagine Parker would allow Antonia to survive until Sunday. Later I would explain to Zeb why I was about to give the same Parker the same gun.

I had a similar idea when I woke up, several hours later, although I wasn't entirely sure how it came into my head. I took the pistol, which wasn't as cold as I expected from being in the freezer, and managed to find my way out without alerting Zeb. He slept late whenever he was worried about something.

If I could find Antonia first I could let her decide how she was going to turn herself in and save Zeb the trouble. I took the shuttle to the university to see if I could catch her. There was nobody else on board. Between robots, and on the straight section of the motorway next to Hospital Bend, the driver read the tiny print from a massive book beside the steering wheel. I wondered if he should be using a magnifying glass.

Instead of Antonia, the first person I encountered at the Institute was Helena Bechman. She had been watching from her office on the second floor of the administration building, and strode down the steps towards me. She meant business, even if the true business of such an institute was catching strange sparks from the language, like glow-worms in a jar. It was Geromian somewhere, I believe, who compared a transport poet to a glow-worm. When you put a glow-worm in a jar, as I once did with Zeb, the Morse code, bright green and pale green, disappeared in minutes.

"I'm looking for Antonia, the agitator you despise. It's important I find her. By any chance you haven't seen her?"

"Neither hide nor hair since last night, when Geromian staged a recovery in her presence. Let's talk further in my office."

"I'm not sure I have the time. I have something urgent."

"Nothing is more urgent than the terms of your employment."

I didn't agree but found myself going across the deserted campus with Helena against my will. The tents had not yet been dismantled but the workshop was chained shut and the Fiat stood unattended. Solly was correct. There was nothing an institute could do to equal five hours on a Golden Arrow bus. Students bumped into us rather than a hundred thousand commuters and thereby their experience was impoverished.

So someone like Antonia, or even Helena, had limited experience of human difference and no practice at tolerating the variety in people's souls. Whereas Solly spent hours in conversation with a schoolgirl from Rustenberg, and the beautician by Obz Café, and the countryside teacher on the taxi who had a chicken with its red feet tied in a box on her lap and could be coaxed into parting with her recipes for chicken stock and chicken knuckles which might, unbeknown to her, find their way into a taxi sonnet.

Solly, I think, would have appreciated my having the gun. Helena could never have imagined something so contrary to her plans. If

I took it out and pointed it at her, she would deny its existence. She would be debating the existence of bullets.

On the steps of the admin building Helena came to the subject on her mind.

"I have talked to the board of directors about your employment. I argued your case, Adam, as far as I saw fit, but I've never seen one word of the snoek poem you were writing when you came here. From what I see, you would be far happier on a proper Hi-Ace than with us. I have seen you at the front of a classroom. You look as if you're being crucified, putting the nails into your own wrists."

"It's my cross, Helena. Why should you, or the board of directors, tell me when to put it down? So you hold me responsible for Geromian's almost overdose. A good taxi poet who's serious about his profession concerns himself with new sensations. Sometimes, yes, that means pills. I didn't force him to take them. But get rid of me if you wish. I may not be guilty but, okay, I am not so very innocent."

"This is as much for your benefit as for the students, Adam. You've been phoning it in for years. For all the problems, you know that you have always been a favourite of Sebastian's. Sebastian always said one didn't hire an elephant for the post in the Department of Zoology. Still you would be the elephant he chose."

I would have said to the Bechmans, if I hadn't been intimidated by their perfect articulateness, that I would have employed this remarkable elephant. Who was to say which was the zoologist and which was the elephant? Solly, on the other hand, might have agreed, arguing that elephants stood apart. However, you wouldn't quote Solly's opinion to either of the Bechmans if you were halfway wise, which I wasn't. But I had to find Antonia.

Helena called me back for a minute. There was a strange light in her eyes, which could have been kindness, or intelligence, or even cruelty.

"The hotel is delivering Geromian to my office in ten minutes. I will send him to find you before he needs to leave for the airport. Do you know, my doctor tells me that our friend has six months to live? Doctors aren't magicians but I believe it. You thought he was shamming all this time. I suppose even shammers have to die."

"We do. I'll wait for Gerome at the gate."

If I missed the Perreira Institute it would be for the view. Cape Town taxi poets are inspired by the city's many such views and changes of perspective. From the gate of the Institute you saw the red roofs in the working-class districts, the old power plant, and the factories and warehouses and train yards in the direction of Paarden Eiland. Behind them were the vague blue teeth of the Hottentots-Holland.

In the near distance was Main Road, endless Main Road leading to Rome and the mountains, along which ran one minibus after another, matchbox cars taking on passengers in front of the internet cafés and chicken-burger palaces and the Bukharinite bookshop.

Even nearer, when I looked away, was Geromian, who was about to return to noble athletic clubs and mountainside favelas, the subject matter of his later taxi poetry. He was better off in Brazil where he would have a supply of tablets if he had to die on instruction of Helena's physician. But I didn't absolve him of his defection. He had left us behind and there was nothing so wrong about us.

"Helena told me you'd be here, Adam. I came out to escape any more of her conversation."

"She's not happy, Gerome. What can I say? She's right. I shouldn't have let you take so many pills yesterday."

"As I said, those red tablets are a placebo, nothing but salt and some vitamins. I have become so wise I can cure myself through the placebo effect. It was Antonia's beauty that overcame me. She is quite exquisite, isn't she, Adam? I might invite her to visit the continent."

I said, "I could almost do that for you, Gerome. She has a particular fascination for older men. But better not. You can't tell me where she went?"

"You could try Maya Rooknodien. I'm not sure. Antonia left after they gave me a sedative and then the whole world vanished. I have something to tell you, however. Your friend Solly will be here as an invisible factor when Maya has turned into dust. He continues to increase the beauty in how people speak and dream, how they see each other and themselves. It's like the loaves and fishes. Someone like Solly is broken up into so many pieces, as many as the people who went on his taxis. Maybe they don't remember him as such. Maybe they can't quote an entire stanza. Maybe they are not familiar with his name. Nonetheless, he is very much alive and acting in the language. That is what I wanted to tell you to cheer you up. The person who suffers most from your unfriendly spirit, after all, is yourself."

It was the most unexpected declaration, a line of Friday's philosophy I never expected from Geromian. I was reluctant to forgive him and would have perpetrated a soul murder on him if I could have, but that he was capable of grace, on occasion, was a true fact. I could almost feel my heart beating out of admiration. I could have loved Geromian, as I could have loved Solly better and more wisely.

"I've never heard you mention another taxi poet favourably, Gerome, unless it was to comment on the lines you say Charlotte Monaghan borrowed without asking."

"Whereas you still don't give anybody a second chance, Ace. Therefore you are a danger to yourself and others. In that way, seeing how you operate, this week has been an education for me."

Was I dangerous? I wasn't as dangerous as Antonia. I could hardly imagine the taxi poems she could write, or what Zeb, my Skywalker, would produce in whatever format. Meanwhile, even if he was fatally ill, Geromian looked like a million dollars. He had borrowed my good health.

"You'll be glad to hear that Helena just fired me. You'll say that I wanted it to happen. Which may be true and all but I haven't been unemployed even for one day since I was fifteen years, do you believe it? Even when I left Parker's company I had a temporary job in the traffic department."

"No, I wanted it to happen," he said. "I told Helena to do it, on the way to the hospital. No proper taxi poet can work in a place like that. Something will turn up for you. Since we're on the subject, did your friend Solly ever force you into the bath with him? He tried it on me once at a trade-union meeting but I turned him down. It didn't stop him from trying a few more times until it became clear that I could wrestle him to a standstill. Whereas you were so close to him, so eager to display the connection between you and himself, that I always assumed there was something more there. I can't help suspecting it may have something to do with the way he met his end."

"Solly had trick knees, you know. I often helped him over the side of the tub. Once he asked me to put talcum powder on his back. So I did that. But no further. As to how he met his end, I cannot say anything. There are too many interests at stake."

"That's your story then, Pudding. Do you want to come to the airport? Make sure I have departed?"

"I would, Gerome. But I have one problem that needs to be straightened out before I can call this week a stalemate between me and the fates. In its way, it's been a pleasure."

"That it has. One last thing I've wanted to say to you. We are the prophets of our own religion of the taxi. That's why people follow us and travel in the company of our dialect. It's the inner meaning of taxi poetry."

So Solly was a prophet also. They were travelling prophets. At a point in time when the transport poem was a decolonising agent, they held a Makarov machine pistol in one hand, a pen in the other. Meanwhile the universe of taxis was changing and disappearing, once a macrocosm, and now a business-friendly microcosm. In my generation we had mere cunning, mere cleverness, mere mobile irony, which came out of the side of the mouth. Whereas true taxi poetry grew out of the primordial instincts of a human being, making sides into new centres. I thought that my secret hatreds of Geromian, and my other secret principles, were my real contribution to the field.

Geromian said, "Find your Zebulon another line of work. He doesn't have the splinter of ice in his heart a taxi poet requires."

"Oh, I fear that he may."

"Up to you to decide. I'll see you, Ace, in one of these worlds. You still have your potential left. I was older than you are now when I did my best work in Portuguese. You promised the world a snoek poem. Write it now. We may yet see it placed on the side of half the buses in São Paulo."

"I figure once I have the first line, the rest will go smoothly."

Before I was ready for the conversation to be over, Geromian was gone. The taxi came by to fetch him and he sprang on board with a boy's lightest step. I had a longing to go with him, accompany him through life, and resent him forever. At the same time I should have liked to erase the letters in his name from my memory. Any taxi poet, and anyone who rode in a taxi, had infinite longings—for perfect love, and friendship, for his lines to be forever on people's lips, for poverty to vanish so that happiness was finally purified. But you learned to take such postponed desires and even make your soul from them. I thought I learned the lesson from Solly yet it might better have come from my own experience.

I should begin with the basics. Solly said that whatever had the least conventional poetry—groceries and clipping for Shoprite coupons and the counter at the petrol station—was the true subject of a transport poet. But that didn't help me.

If I had to be out of love with somebody, and even if that somebody was Solly Greenfields, then I had to be in love with somebody else, and for the reason that a taxi poet had to be transported out of himself. If it wasn't Geromian I was out of love with then it wouldn't be Helena Bechman and maybe not Parker either and certainly not Antonia.

This made me suddenly ardent about Maya Rooknodien. She knew everything and had conquered everyone, including Parker. She could say that life wasn't a beauty contest. There wasn't a motherly bone in her body interrupting her judgement. Apart from anything, Antonia had likely gone to stay with her. Maya could tell me what to do.

I went to find her in Sea Point. Dr Rooknodien's surgery was on the rear side of a tower across from the promenade, where he treated the local women whose children lived in San Diego and Haifa and who were peculiarly, almost sexually, aroused by the gallantry of his manner.

Maya worked from her late-husband's office. You still went past a receptionist's desk, where a guard sat playing a game on his cellphone. You continued along a dank passage hung with drug-company calendars which must have continued to arrive, year after year, as a posthumous present to the doctor who was no longer a prisoner of calendars.

There was a cupboard in the hallway on top of which was a

metal typewriter. You wanted to press the keys. Then you turned around and found yourself in front of Maya, talking on two telephones at once, and wondered if her beauty was going to cut you in the face. She was an injurer with her looks, heedless and reckless, just as I injured Geromian with my conversation, and perhaps Zeb and Solly too.

Maya covered one receiver with a hand, listened on the other line, made some comment, and talked to me between the two proceedings.

"You finally came for Antonia? I thought you would come on Wednesday already, after the Taxi Owners Association. That was when I worked it out and put some pointed questions to Parker. At least you're here. Parker called for her this morning. If you want to ensure she's alive, I'd hurry."

I said, "I am slow to see the connections."

"For a slowcoach, you have a fast mind. It's not just you. Because of his reputation for being a martyr, nobody dreamed of looking sideways at Solly. You never noticed how Solly was flagrant about his liking for young boys and girls, especially these past few years. Some of your Perreira interns come and tell me interesting stories."

"Nobody said a word to me."

"Speaking for myself, I didn't want to take away your hero worship. That's another contradiction, Adam. Despite your sceptical attitudes, you have an even stronger tendency to revere, even when you don't like the individual. It kept you from greatness. Meantime, I instructed Parker to protect your son. He listens to me because I am the only one strong enough to take over from him when he retires. Don't thank me, Adam. Remember that I warned you that something was going on and you didn't listen. Sometimes I agree with Montalban. I don't know why, on top of the Congress Party and the Somalis and Rosenstein and the price of petrol, we need the added headache of you taxi poets."

"You do need us, if only as the memory of a different way of doing things. You may regret it when the memory fades and everything that is left is business."

She stood up with the telephones still in her hands, their long spiral cords stretched tight. For a minute, and it was the first such minute in twenty years of my existence, there was silence between Maya and me and it was filled by my fervent memories of her schoolgirl form. It seemed to me that the green smoke in my head came out of her ring.

I put my arms around Maya while she stood, waited until she put down both of her telephones, and kissed her. I would have fainted into her if I had the strength. I could see that Dr Rooknodien, who ran marathons, didn't have the strength to survive a year around his wife.

Maya wasn't unwilling. But then she pushed me away and looked at me as if she was determining my punishment. She seemed to want to take her telephones again. I was not worthy of her attention now as in school time.

"Thank you for that, Adam. I don't mind your admiration, which has lasted twenty years. But it's just admiration, which doesn't go any further than one of your maybes. Go sort it out with Parker first. Whatever you want to say about a man like Parker, he makes himself responsible for all your difficulties. He has been behind your story all along, although it would kill you to admit it."

Maya was right. Everybody besides me was correct. I had this shopworn, busworn, travelling heart, as out of date as the Toyota Hi-Ace. We could play the fool, or the clown, or set up a road safety council to send out proclamations. But if we were to infringe on any real interests, like a government tender running into the billions, the same freedom wouldn't last one second.

We needed them more than they needed us. Unless Parker

wanted to get me out of it, Zeb and I were in the soup—a scalding hot bowl of alphabet soup. In what other kind would a taxi poet find himself?

There were taxis coming and going from Parker's house, but nobody seemed to notice me. I went through the kitchen and found Antonia at the tiled table there. She was too miserable to be surprised to see me. I sat beside her. She had dish rings around her eyes. I thought if she never slept again that would be a fitting revenge for Solly. At the same time I was surprised that someone so young caused that quantity of disturbance in the world. It should be the battered hearts who created problems.

"You left your problems for Zeb, Antonia."

"He had the choice not to get involved. I didn't put a gun to his head."

"Same difference. You knew Zeb liked you and would do almost anything for you. You have no sense of economy, no proportion. You shot Solly although it wasn't in any way necessary. And you entangled my son in the consequences. I should shoot you right now."

"I didn't intend for it to happen. I trusted Solly because you made a legend out of him. But I have no excuse to change your mind. Parker says he will follow your advice. If you want me to die as a punishment, he is ready to oblige."

"I don't want to explain that decision to my son."

And then Parker was there. I felt as if I had pushed hard on a door and it opened too quickly.

"I talked to Maya already, Parker. Since she didn't care enough to get involved, it must have been your guys who took care of the cottage after Zeb and Antonia left. They were far too amateurish to erase the evidence. Your guys cleaned up the scene, and put

Solly on the couch. The only thing they didn't have was the gun. Why would you cover it up?"

"Sometimes you don't hear how you sound, my friend Adam. You can be absurd, so emotional, and so distanced from the facts. They came to me with a practical problem. I solved it, for the sake of Solly's reputation as much as anybody else's."

"Nobody's explained anything this week."

"I am not sure there is any explanation, except that, once you work for me, you have earned my loyalty. It was for you, and for Zeb, and everything the taxi poets did. As for Solly, I never loved him as a saint, but I prefer for him to die like a saint. Antonia, would you leave us for a minute? Thank you, my dear."

Antonia went out of the room. Parker was happy, as if he had brought me back into the fold. All this time Solly had been a false father. Parker, whom I never chose, turned out to be the true father and hero of my existence. He arranged the solutions to my problems while I pretended to be a part of the resistance. If a taxi poet was a man of twists and turns, mine were on the inside, whereas Parker and Montalban and Maya Rooknodien and Antonia and the Bechmans made their twists and turns in the real world.

Parker went on. "You want her dead, Adam? Say the word and she'll meet with an accident."

"I don't work from the Old Testament, Parker. But Zeb has to be kept out. In my opinion, Antonia may turn out to be the rival of Geromian, and perhaps even Charlotte Monaghan, although greatness is entirely subjective until it's not. She has that kind of will-to-power. Maybe there's a body behind every great career, I don't know."

"I don't believe there has to be punishment in every case. We shall see. Meantime she can work for the company here rather than making trouble at the Road Safety Council. Rest assured that I will keep Zebulon safe as I tried to keep you and Solly Greenfields under protection."

"So do I owe you anything, Parker? Is there something you want from my side?"

"You can send your son to work for me. Or if you prefer, come back to the company yourself. I hear you may not be going back to the Institute."

"Over my dead body. Which doesn't mean I am opposed to friendly relations. Let me give you Antonia's gun, before I forget. A gun makes too much happen. You remember what Solly used to say? Taxi poetry makes nothing happen but that is the very same nothing which makes absolutely everything matter."

"I never heard him say that. Sounds more like you, Adam."

Parker put the gun in his coat, an offering like frankincense and myrrh I was bringing to him on the occasion of a taxi poet's death.

Had it been twenty years since Solly Greenfields stepped into my Hi-Ace on the way to Salt River? I was as rough-skinned as a tattered old yellow tail from swimming among the fifty millions in half a thousand minibus taxis and corner cafés and taxi ranks, from Friday's tales and those First Fridays when the marching clubs drummed along the road in gold-braided uniforms and the Fridays of Rampie-sny, when women cut orange leaves to celebrate the Prophet's birthday and the Friday anniversary of the Revolution of Carnations. It had been on such a Friday when Solly Greenfields recorded a Malay fishing-boat poem on a tape player and saw that you could use the same rhythm for the motor in a Golden Arrow bus.

So my Friday's tale went around and about, like a minibus on Lower Main Road from Observatory to Salt River to Claremont and Rondebosch. There was nobody to say if it had come to a happy ending and I could slide the door open to a new existence.

I could go up to Garib with Zebulon to observe the fields of infinite daisies and the strong brown men in the port, sail through the oil derricks on the Angola seaboard, and board the coal trains burning immense heads of smoke through the high passes.

Maybe the time of the old revolution, which was the time of taxi poetry, was over and we had to leave behind the old forms. Maybe this included taxi poetry itself, which was nothing but one configuration of the travelling mind. The major players in the transport industry had moved beyond the need for taxi poetry. Maya Rooknodien was hard-headed but even the hard heads and the tough hearts could be right on occasion.

I might never write a snoek poem, covering all these grand topics of existence. If I didn't have the fineness of temperament to be a taxi poet, I might write the first taxi novel, a snoek book with a fish in its head like me, and, just like Marmalade, I would cough out the small bones onto the page. For in each of our names, as Solly wrote in a time I could no longer remember and never forget, was contained a story:

For a story is the wind. A story is like the wind,
it comes floating through the air from a far-off place.
For our names are like the wind, and like the wind they float,
they come to people, floating, long before they see us.

ACKNOWLEDGEMENTS

~

Britta Rennkamp, William Dicey, Isobel Dixon, Fourie Botha, Frederik de Jager, Rosa Lyster, Jerry Coovadia, Tara Weinberg, Nasima Badsha, Hedley Twidle, Sadia and Sajedia Essop, Sheikh Hassan Nasrallah, Civitella Ranieri, and Corkie.

The taxi poems on p. 24 and p. 217 use lines from Stephen Watson's "Return of the Moon", and the poem on pp. 113–4 is from his "//Kabbo's Road into Captivity" (*Song of a Broken String*, 1991, Sheep Meadow Press). The poem on p. 24 includes a phrase from Karen Press's "Every Revolution Begins in the Street" (*The Canary's Songbook*, 2005, Carcanet Press). The line on p. 45 is by Keroapetse Kgositsile from the poem "Mayibuye iAfrika" (*If I Could Sing*, 2002, Kwela). The poem on p. 76 adapts lines from Douglas Livingstone's "Love", from the Shona of Wilson Chivaura (*A Ruthless Fidelity: the collected poems of Douglas Livingstone*, 1999, Jonathan Ball). Lines are reprinted with permission.

A NOTE ABOUT THE TYPE

This book is set in Sabon, a typeface designed by Jan
Tschichold in 1964. It was originally a metal type for
hand and machine composition. Sabon is based on the
work of Claude Garamond, a sixteenth-century French
typecutter, and on that of his pupil Jacques Sabon, who
repaired and completed a set of Garamond's punches
after his death.

Green-eyed Thieves

Imraan Coovadia

Green-eyed Thieves

is in a space and maybe a class of its own ... A real treat

<small>CHRIS DUNTON, *THE SUNDAY INDEPENDENT*</small>

SHORTLISTED FOR THE *SUNDAY TIMES* FICTION PRIZE

A mind-boggling tale of inspired crime and brotherly betrayal told by Firoze Peer – amateur philosopher and mystic, artful memoirist, green-eyed conspirator. Born into a crooked Johannesburg family, Firoze and his identical twin brother, Ashraf, are employed from an early age in the family business, where Firoze keeps the books and Ashraf's talent for drawing is put to use in the diamond trade to create counterfeit certificates of rare artistry. From such beginnings, the brothers' lives progress through experiences that span the globe: from a masterful heist at Sun City to a wild pursuit on the Pakistan border to appearing at the White House under false pretences. *Green-eyed Thieves* has everything a reader could want: fast-paced action, a startling conclusion, and an investigation of the most frightening idea that Firoze can imagine: the idea that all men are brothers.

ISBN: 978-1-4152-0009-4 (PRINT)
ISBN: 978-1-4152-0258-6 (EPUB)
ISBN: 978-1-4152-0259-3 (PDF)

Fiction | January 2007
222 mm x 146 mm | 208 pages

To buy online, choose a QR code to scan with your cellphone, or go to www.kalahari.net or www.exclus1ves.co.za

www.randomstruik.co.za   Exclusive Books   Kalahari.net

UMUZI

Also from Umuzi

High Low In-between

Imraan Coovadia

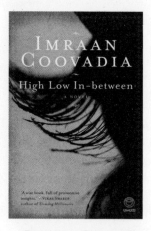

WINNER OF THE *SUNDAY TIMES* FICTION PRIZE AND THE UNIVERSITY OF JOHANNESBURG LITERARY AWARD

"There was nothing in the room to surprise her. She could understand exactly what had happened. She had known about this in the morning. She had known about it the day before, the month before, and in fact since the moment of her birth."

The violent death of her biologist husband forces Nafisa into a world of illegal organ transplants, bribery, and scientific and political controversy. With an acute sense of the disruptions of contemporary South Africa, and its keen feeling for love and loss, *High Low In-between* reveals Nafisa's relationships with the people close to her and the anarchic currents of life and death she discovers.

Imraan Coovadia has a unique and marvellously talented voice. High Low In-between *effortlessly extended my capacity to imagine the moral inner world of the kind of character I often wonder about.*

ANTJIE KROG

ISBN: 978-1-4152-0070-4 (PRINT)
ISBN: 978-1-4152-0262-3 (EPUB)
ISBN: 978-1-4152-0263-0 (PDF)

Fiction | June 2009
222 mm x 146 mm | 268 pages

www.randomstruik.co.za

To buy online, choose a QR code to scan with your cellphone, or go to www.kalahari.net or www.exclus1ves.co.za

Exclusive Books

Kalahari.net

UMUZI